PIONEER SPIRIT
Book Two: Indian Affairs

Earle Jay Goodman

Also by Earle Jay Goodman

DISCREET – Book One: Childhood's End
DISCREET – Book Two: Growing Pains
DISCREET – Book Three: Round Up

PIONEER SPIRIT - Book One: Overland Trail
PIONEER SPIRIT - Book Two: Indian Affairs
PIONEER SPIRIT - Book Three: Wars and Rumors
PIONEER SPIRIT - Book Four: An Uneasy Peace
PIONEER SPIRIT - Book Five: White Indians
PIONEER SPIRIT - Book Six: Perilous Times
PIONEER SPIRIT – Book Seven: War Drums

To see photographs and maps of actual historical people and places
during the time of Connal Lee's story, please visit:

https://goodmans-pioneer-spirit.blogspot.com

"...and the desert shall rejoice, and blossom as the rose."

Isaiah 35:1

PIONEER SPIRIT
Book Two: Indian Affairs

Earle Jay Goodman

Dedication

Boca Raton, Florida
2018

    I dedicate this book with love and gratitude to my wonderful parents and grandparents, on both sides of my family, who raised me on the stories of my great and great-great-grandparents, some of the earliest pioneers and settlers of America's Intermountain West in the mid-1800's;

    and, to my friend and advisor since 1973, mentor, and de facto book editor, Edward P. Frey, Esq. – Thanks, Ed;

    and, last but not least, to my first real love since 1979, then business partner, then domestic partner, and now married partner, James John Goodman. You are the light of my life. I love you, Jim.

---Earle Jay Goodman

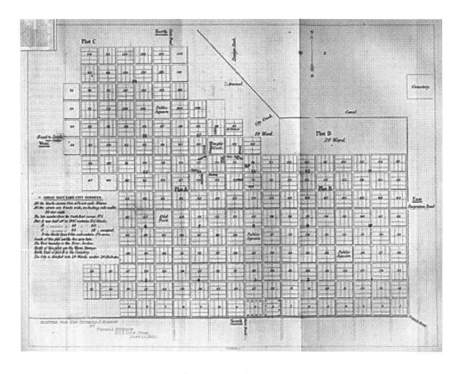

*Map of Great Salt Lake City
in the time of Pioneer Spirit.
The original City stretched
from 8th North to 9th South,
and from 9th West to 8th East,
for a total of 135 Blocks.*

*Population in 1860 Census:
Great Salt Lake City – 8,236
Salt Lake County – 11,295
Territory of Utah – 40,273*

Table of Contents

Chapter 1: Missing Connal Lee

Around 6:30 the evening after the Cavalry joined the handcart train, Captain Hanover ordered the company to pull off and set up camp near an unnamed stream of water. Captain Reed ordered his troops to set up their pup tents about thirty feet out from the handcart camp, surrounding them on all sides. "Lieutenant Anderson, after setting up your camps, have one of your sections take all the horses downstream. Stake them out where they can reach grass and water. Set a rotating guard even across the creek. Then divide up your remaining squads into rotating guard duty during the night, walking the perimeter of the entire encampment. Assign three men to sleep without standing guard duty so they can get up before dawn and ride ahead. I want them to spread out and scout the trail in front of us to make sure we don't ride into any trouble. Tomorrow night, I'll have my squad take a turn at guard duty."

"Yes, sir!"

"When you have the men in order, come join me in the handcart camp. I'll either be with Captain Hanover or with the Swinton family."

"Very good, sir. Right away, sir. Thank you, sir."

Dusk settled over the now quiet camp. The ladies gathered beside the supply wagons to begin cooking a communal supper. Captain Reed ordered his men assigned to cook for the patrol to join them. When the soldiers arrived with more food, they exchanged noisy rounds of introductions before the camp fell quiet as everyone focused on their work. With inevitable sighs, the two privates ordered to peel the potatoes sat down on the ground, knives in hand, and sent a flurry of potato peels flying through the air.

The ambulatory men and boys fetched water to the hospital wagon and the cooking fires. Lorna Baines met the doctor and surgeon's mate at the hospital wagon, where they attended to the wounded. When Captain Reed sought out Captain Hanover just as dark settled in, he found him by the support wagons speaking with Lorna Baines. The Cavalry captain shifted a small yellowed canvas package to his left hand, then stepped up and shook hands with Captain Hanover and Lorna Baines. "Good evening, Captain Hanover. Lovely to see you again, Missus Baines."

Captain Hanover shook hands with a firm grip. "Ah, Captain. Glad ya could join us. We were jus' thinkin' about moseyin' over t' visit Sister Swinton's tent. Brother Swinton told me she's pretty depressed about Baby Boy – Connal Lee. She's jus' sittin' there mopin'. Let's go see if we can cheer 'er up, shall we?"

"Excellent, Captain. I am anxious to hear the whole story of how Connal Lee went missing. I share your concern for my young friend, whom I affectionately called little brother back in Fort Laramie. I was looking forward to discussing books with him again."

Captain Reed offered his arm to Lorna Baines. She laid her hand in the bend of his elbow. They followed Captain Hanover through to the north side of the camp.

When Zeff saw them walking towards his little campfire, he stood up, then reached down and pulled Sister Woman to stand beside him. She held Chester Ray over her left shoulder. Zeff put his arm around her shoulders and pulled her into a hug. After rounds of handshakes and polite greetings, Zeff gestured everyone to take a seat around his little firepit. Gilbert Baines saw them and strode over to join the conversation. Lorna scuttled back to her handcart to find a blanket to sit on. When she returned, Lieutenant Anderson strolled up carrying a small package wrapped in brown paper and tied with a string.

They all settled in with friendly nods and smiles. The flickering flames of the small mesquite fire reflected in their eyes. Captain Reed peered at Zeff, then at Captain Hanover. "So, please tell me everything you know. How did Connal Lee come to be separated from your company?"

Zeff looked at Captain Hanover. The Captain nodded for Zeff to answer. "Well, suh. A while back, we was gettin' hungry fer some fresh game. But night after night, we returned empty-handed from our usual huntin' after we stopped fer the day. There jus' weren't no game close tuh the trail in this here desert. So, Connal Lee came up with the idear o' him headin' out ever mornin' tuh ride up in the hills. Captain Hanover lent 'im a good mount an' a packhorse. Some days 'e did real good. Though once in a while, 'e returned with nothin' fer the pot."

Sister Woman began sniffling, which drew everyone's eyes over to her. She gently set Chester Ray on the ground beside her, tucked his scrap of quilt over him, then dropped her face to both hands. "Ah'm sorry. But Ah miss Baby Boy so, so much."

Zeff scooted over close enough to put his arm around her again. "The day those damn Crow braves attacked us on the road started out jus' like any other day. Connal Lee rode out towards the western range that day, headin' out on 'is usual huntin' trip. Last Ah saw 'im, he rode over the foothills an' disappeared outta sight. It was what, oh, about the same time as we got organized an' hit the road jus' like we do every mornin'. Only them Injuns rode out from around the hill ahead of us an' rode us down. They started shootin' arrows an' a whoopin' an' a shoutin' an' a carryin' on somethin' fierce. We was all scared plumb tuh death. That war party circled around us an' shot us up pretty dang good. Captain Hanover led the men what had weapons tuh defend the camp. They did a good job, all of 'em. After what seemed like ferever, they finally rode off. They came down on us from the east, but they rode off goin' west, pretty much in the same direction Connal Lee had takin'. We're plumb worried they might o' run 'im down out there in the mountains. Who knows what could o' happened tuh 'im."

Zeff shook his head, imagining all the horrible things that might have befallen his little brother. Everyone frowned, worry clearly evident on their faces. Captain Hanover looked over at Captain Reed and Lieutenant Anderson. "Ya see, men, we were plumb busy tendin' our wounded under the kind direction o' Sister Baines, here. I set everyone to tightenin' up the camp, then set up a system o' guards fer the rest o' the day an' that night. Everyone was too beat up an' hurtin' t' leave fer the next couple o' days. While the wounded rested up an' started healin', the rest of us reorganized the supply wagons so Sister Baines could have 'er hospital wagon. Everyone pitched in to cover fer the wounded. We all kept expectin' t' see Connal Lee ridin' in from up the trail, lookin' fer us. But 'e never did. Problem is, that was four days ago, now. He should o' found us by now if 'e were able."

Zeff spoke up. "He's a smart kid, doncha know, plus 'e had 'is compass, too. He would o' figured out that we were behind 'im when we didn't show up down the trail at the end o' the day. Yes, suh, 'e would o' thought 'is way through it an' found us by now, if'n 'e was able. Ah'm so afraid somethin' happened tuh 'im. Ah cain't stand the thought o' me poor little brover out there all alone, maybe wounded or dyin'."

Sister Woman began sobbing loudly, interrupting the conversation. Zeff pulled her face down to his chest and patted her on the back, trying to offer her some comfort. The lieutenant turned to Captain Hanover. "Did you send out a search party, Captain?"

Captain Hanover shook his head with a sad look on his face. "Lieutenant, we were short o' horses. We only had two saddles left. We were short o' men who could ride. Much as I wanted t' lead a search party, meself, we had t' stick together fer protection an' t' tend t' the wounded. I couldn't see anything else t' do. I felt real bad about it, though. Tough decisions. Tough times."

Captain Reed glared angrily at Captain Hanover but held his tongue. Captain Hanover had command, not him or the army. He leaned forward and rested his elbows on his knees. "So, he's a little more than a day's journey back along the Overland Trail, and he's been gone for over four days. Plus, who knows how far north and west he managed to ride that day or since. Even with a full company of men, that leaves us a huge amount of territory to cover if we were to mount a search party."

He looked Captain Hanover in the face, then nodded his head. "Plus, any men we sent out would leave us short of optimal protection here. If I sent out too few, they could be at risk from packs of renegade Indians roaming the countryside. If I sent out enough for them to be safe, we couldn't guard your handcart train properly. Damn it all!"

"Ya see me dilemma, then, doncha, Captain? No matter what I could figure out, I couldn't come up with a good solution all around. Right or wrong, I prayed on it an' chose t' keep the main body o' me company together an' safe. Tough decisions. Tough times."

They all fell silent. Lorna picked up the edge of her long apron and wiped tears from her eyes.

Lieutenant Anderson held out his paper-wrapped package to Zeff. "I remember Connal Lee telling me how much he enjoyed reading *Oliver Twist*. So I thought he might enjoy this book. It's my favorite book by Dickens. *Nicholas Nickleby.* I brought it along for him since he complained he didn't have anything new to read."

Lorna smiled warmly. "He would really have enjoyed it, Lieutenant. You would not believe how he immersed himself in *The Count of Monte Christo*. He surely did enjoy it. It opened up whole new worlds to him. He often said he wished he could have thanked you in person for leaving it for him."

"I'm glad to hear that, Missus Baines. Here, Mister Swinton. Please take this book and keep it for when he shows up. I know things look bleak right now, but I have faith that he is clever enough to survive and find his way back to you."

"Why, thanks, Lieutenant. He will love readin' another story by Dickens, Ah'm sure. Mighty neighborly o' y'all."

Captain Reed coughed into his hand. "It appears we were all thinking the same thing, Lieutenant. Here Mister Swinton. I brought Connal Lee my own favorite book, *The Three Musketeers*. I hoped he would like to read a rousing adventure story about a young man growing up to become a soldier. He seemed interested in everything having to do with soldiering when I met him. Please keep it for him. I found a scrap of canvas waterproofed with boiled oil and wrapped it for him so it would stay dry. I hope he enjoys it. Please tell him I will expect to discuss this novel with him the next time I see him. I agree with the good lieutenant. Connal Lee is smart enough to think his way out of whatever difficulty he finds himself in. I'm sure he will return to you as soon as he can. Good night, everyone. I'm going to take my leave to go check that my men are in good order for the night."

When he stood up, Lieutenant Anderson also rose to his feet. "Good night, friends. I'm so sorry about Connal Lee going missing. If I may, I will accompany you on your rounds, sir."

"Certainly. I would welcome the company, Lieutenant."

Captain Hanover stood up next. "Well. I think I'll make my own rounds an' seek out my bed at the end of 'em. Good night, Brother an' Sister Swinton. Pleasant dreams, Brother an' Sister Baines."

The Swintons and Baines sat, two sad couples snuggled in each other's arms, staring into the fire as the flames dwindled. Finally, Gilbert stood up and offered a hand to pull Lorna to her feet. She bent back down and picked up her blanket. "Good night, Brother Swinton. Good night, Sister Swinton."

"Good night, y'all."

Chapter 2: Desert Survival Course

The small Shoshone family and Connal Lee saddled up their horses to continue their mission to keep an eye on the Crow war party. The beautifully beaded and fringed saddles the three natives put on their large war steeds fascinated Connal Lee. The front and back of their saddles looked almost like Connal Lee's saddle horn but taller, with one rising in front and one behind the seat.

Screaming Eagle tied his war bonnet over his long black hair. Delicate downy eagle feathers tied to the tips of the large eagle wing feathers standing up around his bonnet, fluttering on the slightest breeze or movement made by Screaming Eagle. Connal Lee found it very beautiful.

They loaded up their three packhorses and rode northeast away from their campground. Screaming Eagle had ridden this path before, so he confidently led the way. They made good time on their strong well-rested mounts. However, about the time they stopped for a noon break, Connal Lee felt his strength waning. He also discovered that his forehead, cheeks, and nose were becoming sunburned without his big felt hat. After they dismounted and ate a cold travel meal, Connal Lee pointed out how the red skin on his face.

White Wolf peered closely. "Now I understand why white man wear hat all time. Skin burn. We Newe no burn. We like sun. The sun like us."

Short Rainbow touched his cheek, leaving a white fingerprint on the sunburned skin. "Need hat. Need salve for burn."

White Wolf nodded his agreement and turned to Screaming Eagle. In Shoshone, he told him they would make camp here, but he should ride ahead and check on the Crow war party. He then pointed at Connal Lee. "Please. Unsaddle packhorses. Make fire. I back quick."

White Wolf leapt up on his war stallion and galloped away. He watched for prickly pear cactus out away from the little stream they had stopped beside, where the desert was arid enough for them to survive. He found a small cluster of green and red cacti, bristling with long needle-sharp spines. He carefully cut off three large pads with his steel knife and pushed them into a small deer hide medicine pouch.

When White Wolf returned to the camp, he dumped the cactus pads directly into the flames of the fire. He picked up a stick, then knelt upwind from the smoke to watch the cactus carefully. Once he saw that all the dangerous spines and the tough outer skins of the pads had burned off, he flicked the denuded pads out of the flames. Short Rainbow brought him their gourd bowl from the packhorses and placed it on the ground beside him. White Wolf nodded his thanks. He carefully squeezed the slippery juice out of the cactus into the bowl, then tossed the pulp back into the fire. "Connal Lee. Come. Please."

Connal Lee walked over and sat down Indian-style on the ground beside him. White Wolf reached out his hand and turned Connal Lee's face towards him with a smile. "Red! Now you red man. Ha!"

White Wolf dipped his fingers into the slippery cactus salve and gently spread it over Connal Lee's exposed skin. "Help. Medicine. For burns."

Connal Lee nodded that he understood. "Thank you. Aeshen."

Short Rainbow danced over with a piece of leather in her hands. She wrapped the edge around Connal Lee's cranium and measured the start of a cap. Using a piece of charcoal from the fire, she marked where to cut. When Connal Lee looked at her, puzzled, she twittered a bright laugh. "Make war bonnet white man style." Then she asked in Shoshone, as she shaded her eyes with her hand, "How do you say make shade to cover the face? Shade?"

White Wolf and Connal Lee both answered her at the same time in English. "Shade."

She nodded happily. A few minutes later, she returned with a strip of leather about four inches wide and twenty-two inches long and held it around Connal Lee's head. In Shoshone, she explained, "I'm going to make a hat like an extra big war bonnet, only this bonnet will be topped with a solid crown without eagle feathers. Then, with a brim sewn around the base of the bonnet, Connal Lee will have a Sho-shone style white man hat."

White Wolf leaned over and gave her a hug. "So clever. How can I help?"

"Get an awl and make holes to bind the ends together while I cut the crown to top off the bonnet. The bonnet will also need holes along the bottom to attach the brim and along the top to attach the crown."

Somehow, through watching their gestures and picking up the odd word, Connal Lee understood they were making him a replacement hat. He felt awkward not contributing. "White Wolf, I want to help. I don't want you doing everything for me."

White Wolf and Short Rainbow looked at each other with their eyebrows raised. White Wolf shook his head no. "Too much time teach. We do. You good hunt with rifle?"

Connal Lee brightened up. "Yes. I'm good at tracking and hunting. How about if I ride out and find some fresh meat for our supper while you make my hat?"

"Yes. Good. But ride away from Crow. No follow Screaming Eagle."

"I understand. Of course. I wouldn't want the Crow to hear my rifle."

Full of renewed energy at having something to do to contribute to the camp, he strode over, tightened the cinch, and mounted his dark brown mare. He waved cheerfully. "I'll be back as soon as I can."

White Wolf and Short Rainbow waved as he turned the mare around and trotted away, pulling his packhorse behind him.

About an hour later, he spotted a flock of ring-necked pheasants scrounging for seeds in a grassy stretch of land. He nearly missed the well-camouflaged females against the dried grass and weeds, but the brilliant iridescent blue neck feathers and the stark white ring around the males' necks made them easy to see. He quickly pulled out his shotgun and switched out the lead balls for buckshot. With two quick shots directly into the flock, he managed to bring down a large cock and four smaller hens. The rest of the flock flew off in a big whoosh! With a proud smile, Connal Lee pulled a leather string from his pants pocket, tied the birds together by their necks, and draped them over the packsaddle.

He arrived back in camp, quite exhausted – to his surprise – but happy with the hunt. White Wolf noticed Connal Lee's exhaustion and recommended he rest for a while. White Wolf spread out one of his sleeping furs and gestured for Connal Lee to relax on it. Short

Rainbow immediately seized the male pheasant, chattering happily in Shoshone about how she wanted to harvest the lovely feathers. White Wolf could pluck, gut, and prepare the females for frying. She didn't care about their dull brown and tan feathers.

By the time Screaming Eagle rode back into camp, Connal Lee proudly wore a neatly sewn leather hat. White Wolf sat beside the fire, frying pheasants for their supper. Short Rainbow sat bowed over her lap, humming a meditation while she crafted a hatband for Connal Lee's new hat out of gorgeous pheasant feathers. She finished it with a three-inch rondel of short, brilliant blue neck feathers to cover the seam where the two ends joined around the hat's crown. Connal Lee shook his head in amazement at her talents and ability to work so fast. "That's plumb beautiful, Short Rainbow. Plumb beautiful. Ah really don't know how y'all do it. Thanks so much. Ah thank y'all, too, White Wolf. Wow!"

Screaming Eagle asked Connal Lee to teach him how to shoot a rifle while they waited for supper. Both White Wolf and Short Rainbow objected, complaining they wanted to learn, too. He gave in to their requests and offered to teach Connal Lee how to shoot a hunting bow. They stepped away from the camp. Screaming Eagle stood behind Connal Lee and instructed him on the correct way to stand, how to nock and hold the arrow, how to aim up a bit higher than the target to compensate for the downward arc of the arrow in flight, and how to adjust for wind. Connal Lee didn't understand all the words, but he caught on quickly. Before it became too dark to shoot, they collected the arrows and returned to the campfire.

As they ate supper, Screaming Eagle complimented Connal Lee on his hunting. Connal Lee thanked him for the shooting lesson. "One good thing about your bows and arrows is that you can make and reuse your arrows. Once I shoot a bullet, it is gone. I need civilization for more ammunition. You know, to buy gunpowder, shot, and lead for casting balls."

The group discussed this problem. White Wolf decided only Screaming Eagle would actually shoot the rifle in practice so they could save their ammunition for hunting and self-defense. White Wolf and Short Rainbow agreed to practice without live ammunition for the time being. "Connal Lee. No problem find lead, find shot.

We find Fort Hall. Trade. We give fur. Trader give shot, lead. Trade good. When hunt tomorrow, watch for fur *and* for food."

They had a lively conversation about the most valuable furs. None of them had English words for fox, marten, mink, otter, or beaver pelts, the most highly valued for trade. "Besides," as White Wolf pointed out, "We no find here. Here deer, bear, wolf. No worry. We trade. We get bullets."

The temperature fell quickly after the sun went down behind the hills to their west, so they all snuggled up together on their blankets. Connal Lee noticed his friends making love beneath the sleeping furs. He smiled, happy that his friends loved each other. He fell asleep thinking, *Someday Ah will have someone to love, too. Someday...*

Chapter 3: As The Crow Flies

For the next several days, Connal Lee rode north and east with the young Shoshone family. The days reached a comfortable sixty degrees, but the nights cooled down to nearly forty. They rode steadily between sunrise at seven-thirty and sunset around seven. They alternated between a mile-eating two-beat trot where they averaged ten miles an hour and a four-beat walk at four miles an hour. Every hour brought them closer to Crow lands centered in the mountains that the early French trappers had named Roche Jaune. When Lewis and Clark visited the area in 1805, they translated Roche Jaune and noted their maps and journals with the name Yellow Stone, which became the name of both the river and its valley.

One afternoon Screaming Eagle called out to wait. They reined in their horses and watched as he hopped off his war steed. He looked around at the sere dry ground. White Wolf dismounted his stallion and walked over. "What is it, Screaming Eagle?"

Screaming Eagle pointed to tracks in the ground. "It looks as if the war party split up here. Most continued north like we expected, but a few turned back west."

"Hm. Why would they do that?"

"I don't know, White Wolf. But I think we better find out. I think I should follow the group that went west while you follow the main party, at least for today."

"I don't like the idea of us splitting up."

"I don't either, but we need to know what they are doing. We don't want them to return and cause mischief to our people." Screaming Eagle looked up at the angle of the sun. "Let me ride out for two hours and see what I can learn, then I'll ride back and meet you north of here. When I reach about twenty miles out, I'll turn back. If you continue north at an easy walk, I can meet you in time for supper."

White Wolf thought it over. "Very well. We'll be ten or twelve miles north of here preparing supper. Be cautious. Be alert."

Screaming Eagle put his big hand on White Wolf's shoulder and gave him an affectionate shake. "I'm always cautious and alert. You worry too much."

White Wolf just shook his head. "Hurry back."

An hour before sunset Connal Lee rode off to find something for their supper. White Wolf and Short Rainbow set up camp for the evening. Connal Lee returned with a young mountain goat, already cleaned where he shot it. He worked with White Wolf and Short Rainbow to skin it and carve off the lean meat. Short Rainbow put the diced meat in a small metal pot to stew with fistfuls of dried corn, dried squash, and dried herbs.

They waited for Screaming Eagle to return. Connal Lee and White Wolf practiced conversation. Connal Lee spoke only in Shoshone. White Wolf spoke only in English. Sometimes they had to smile when their discussion sounded like baby talk. Finally, White Wolf stood up and scanned anxiously south and west, hoping to find Screaming Eagle riding towards them. "No good Screaming Eagle late. I worry."

Connal Lee stood up and patted White Wolf on the back as he responded in Shoshone, "No worry. He strong. He good."

Short Rainbow rose gracefully to her feet. "Actually, I don't like that he's late, either. He promised to return in time for supper. Something must have happened."

They all stood frowning. A vagrant gust of wind blew smoke around them. Connal Lee wiped a tear from his eye after receiving a face full of sagebrush smoke. They stood looking into the distance as full dark descended over their little camp. Short Rainbow invited them to eat supper while they waited.

Hours dragged by. No Screaming Eagle. They snuggled up in sleeping furs for warmth as the temperature quickly dropped. After they lay there an hour, Short Rainbow sat up. "I can't sleep. Sorry. I just know something has happened to Screaming Eagle. Either an accident or the Crow warriors stopped him. I think we should ride out and find him."

White Wolf sat up in their furs. "We can't track him in a moonless night like this, Short Rainbow. Let's rest a little longer. We'll get up and start just before dawn if he hasn't returned by then and go find him. Come. Give me a hug. I'm freezing."

After they pulled a buffalo hide blanket over them, Connal Lee snuggled up to White Wolf. His hand reached over and patted Short

Rainbow's arm, comforting her as best he could. However, Connal Lee began worrying and couldn't fall back to sleep. He rolled over onto his back and gazed up at the twinkling stars with the Milky Way clearly visible behind them.

They all seemed to wake up at the same time. Only the barest hint of light could be seen on the underside of the clouds to their east. Without a word, they began saddling their horses and loading the packhorses. They didn't pause to prepare any hot tea or food. They only drank some water from their water bags before taking off at a fast trot. The sun rose, lighting the way for them to inspect the ground for signs of riders.

Connal Lee had always had a sharp eye when it came to tracking. He spotted white feathers on the ground beside a short sagebrush before the others and pulled his horse aside to investigate. From a hundred feet away, he identified the feathers as a war bonnet. "There! Look! Isn't that Screaming Eagle's bonnet?"

Short Rainbow rushed over to look. "I knew something bad happened to him. I just knew it!"

White Wolf hopped down off his tall horse and slowly walked closer, checking out the ground to see what signs could be determined from footprints in the sandy soil. He pointed at a small outcropping of jagged granite not too far away. "It appears the Crow party he was tracking ambushed him from behind those rocks. I don't see sign of blood, but somehow they managed to capture him."

Short Rainbow stifled her anger and fear. Connal Lee pulled his rifle out of its sheath and loaded lead slugs. White Wolf and Short Rainbow both strung their war bows and retrieved barbed arrows from their store on a packhorse. Everyone mounted up in a businesslike manner. Connal Lee led the way, watching the ground carefully to follow the trail. He easily followed the twelve or thirteen hours old prints not yet blurred from wind or rain. As he rode, he asked White Wolf and Short Rainbow to keep watch in the distance so he could focus on the tracks in the sandy soil. When the trail led over a hill, Connal Lee stopped. "We can't go riding blindly over the hill. We don't know how many Crow warriors there are, but if they see us outlined against the sky, they will know we are coming and either hide or attack."

White Wolf answered in Shoshone. "You are wise in this strategy. Please go stealthily and check out the path ahead. We will follow when you give us the all-clear."

Connal Lee dismounted and handed his reins to White Wolf. He walked up the gentle incline until he nearly reached the top, then he squatted down, then he dropped down to his hands and knees. He crawled the last ten feet, keeping as low to the ground as possible. He poked his head up just enough to see down the other side of the hill.

He found five Crow warriors finishing up their breakfast beside a tiny smokeless cookfire. With a catch in his throat, he spotted Screaming Eagle tied up with leather ropes with his arms bound behind him and his hands tied to his feet. It looked like an unnatural and painful contortion. Screaming Eagle lay on his side with eyes wide open. Connal Lee breathed a sigh of relief when Screaming Eagle took a deep breath. The small war party stood up and began saddling their horses. One kicked at the fire to put it out.

Connal Lee scurried backward until far enough below the ridge to stand up. He ran down the hill in a panic, stifling the urge to call out his news. He jumped on his beautiful mare, turned her head towards Short Rainbow and White Wolf, and moved in close. Keeping his voice low, he recounted what he had discovered. After a brief discussion, White Wolf made up his mind. "They won't be expecting us. They will be busy getting ready to ride rather than watching the crest of the hill. We'll sneak up to the top. Connal Lee, you take out two of those vile Crow kidnappers in the middle of the group. Short Rainbow, you take the warrior on the far right. I'll take the one on the far left. That way, we won't waste our first shots on the same man. Then, we'll all fire on the remaining skunk until they are all dead."

Connal Lee pulled back in alarm. His hands began quivering. "But, White Wolf, Ah've never shot a man before."

"It's just hunting, Connal Lee. Only this time, you hunt the most vicious predators on the plains, men. We have to get them before they get us. If they think we might rescue Screaming Eagle, they will kill him immediately to prevent it. We have to attack fast and accurately. Now, bring your weapons. It's time to rescue Screaming Eagle. When we reach the crest, we'll load up, then I'll quietly count to three.

On the count of three, we all stand and shoot at the same time. Understood?"

Connal Lee checked to make sure his rifle had bullets. Short Rainbow pulled her lovely beaded quiver over to her left shoulder so she could reach the sharp war arrows with her right hand. She nocked an arrow and began stomping angrily up the hill. Connal Lee and White Wolf soon caught up to her. They dropped down to crawl the last fifteen feet so they could look over the top of the low hill.

"One."

"Two."

"Three."

Two bullets slammed into the busy warriors at the same time that two arrows took out two more of the enemy. The unwounded warrior jerked around in surprise to identify the threat, only to receive two arrows in his chest almost immediately. One by one, the Crow raiders collapsed to the ground. More arrows followed as they made doubly sure they had killed all five hated Crow enemies. Short Rainbow took off running towards Screaming Eagle. He lay tied up on his side, watching their attack with eyes opened wide in astonishment. Short Rainbow pulled out her antler-handled volcanic glass knife and cut the ropes binding his hands and feet. Then she pulled the chamois rag out of his mouth. She began chafing her hands over Screaming Eagle's swollen red hands to restore circulation. White Wolf finished checking the fallen, ensuring they were all dead. Then he ran over, dropped to his knees, and began rubbing Screaming Eagle's swollen ankles.

Connal Lee knelt down and gently lifted Screaming Eagle's head. He held out his water bag so Screaming Eagle could take a sip of water. Finally, Screaming Eagle coughed as he pulled his hands away from Short Rainbow. He pushed his long hair back off his face with both hands. One of his braids had come loose when his bonnet was knocked off his head. He reached up and cringed when he felt a bloody swelling on the top back of his head. "You surprised me how you came out of nowhere to attack those scum raiders. But you sure are a welcome sight. Thank you for coming to my rescue. How did you manage to track me so quickly?"

White Wolf patted Connal Lee on the back. "Connal Lee tracked you. We just tagged along to lend him support." He stopped talking and gazed hard at Connal Lee's face. Still speaking in Shoshone, he asked, "How are you doing there, Connal Lee?"

Connal Lee stood trembling with his face pulled into a frown. He kept his eyes averted from the dead men on the other side of the firepit. White Wolf pulled him into a big hug. Short Rainbow understood the turmoil he felt from killing his first human beings. She went over and embraced him, as well. Screaming Eagle knelt up and pulled them all into a group hug. He whispered in English, "Thank you. You save life. I grateful long time. Thank you, Connal Lee."

Connal Lee broke down in tears. "I had to do it. I know that. But it was awful."

Screaming Eagle pulled them all in tighter and patted Connal Lee on his back. "No cry. Victory. Heap big success. You rescue. Me grateful. No cry."

After a few more minutes, Connal Lee settled down. Their group hug broke up. Short Rainbow and White Wolf helped Screaming Eagle to his feet. White Wolf carefully examined Screaming Eagle to see what injuries he had suffered when captured. He inspected the big lump on his head. "Let's get to the horses and find some water. I want to clean that broken scalp and get us all something to eat. Screaming Eagle, how did they manage to capture you, anyway?"

"One of them threw his tomahawk from behind. It not only knocked me out, it knocked me off my horse. I didn't have a chance to fight or run. It was dark by the time I came to, and they had me securely tied up. I struggled at the ropes for most of the night but couldn't get them to budge."

They walked briskly up over the hill. Connal Lee didn't look back at the scene of the rescue. After they started down the other side, White Wolf stopped. "You go on ahead. I'm going back for our arrows and the Crow horses. Ride due west and keep your eyes out for water. I'll catch up."

White Wolf finished packing up the dead Crows' horses and possessions. He grabbed their reins, hopped up on his warhorse, and led them over the hill. He followed his spouses, who had a good hour start on him. Determined to catch up, he spurred the horses into a trot. Some resisted, but he yanked their reins until they fell into order.

White Wolf soon caught up with his family. They rode together until they found a campsite.

Chapter 4: Snake River Basin

On a cold fall day in the first week of November 1857, Captain Hanover led the handcart company up and over a rise. They saw Fort Hall in the distance. Its stout white plaster walls built twenty years earlier for the fur trade now protected travelers on the Overland Trail. The weary handcart company found it a welcome sight.

Captain Hanover ordered the company to make camp between the Fort and the Snake River. The tributaries and meandering tree-lined feeder creeks of the mighty Snake River softened the harsh desert.

The company didn't like finding smoke-blackened tipis not far up the river from the fort, obviously a large camp of nomad Indians.

Captain Reed commanded Lieutenant Anderson to set up their camp downstream from the Mormon pioneers. He ordered his troops to rest two nights before setting out on the return trip to Fort Laramie. The captain strode into the Fort to report their arrival and catch up on the news of the trail.

Soldiers stationed at the Fort came out to meet the handcart train. Zeff struck up a conversation with gruff old Sergeant McCall. They introduced themselves. "Howdy! Ah'm Zefford Ray Swinton. Jus' call me Zeff."

"I'm Sergeant McGraw, young feller. At yer service."

The conversation soon turned to the Shoshone clan camped not too far away. Sergeant McGraw grinned toothlessly. "Theys jus' here t' trade their fur pelts fer metal stuff an' fer beads. Don't yas worry none, youngun, theys peaceful. These here're what we call *good* Injuns, these here Shoshones. Theys not like some o' the other tribes like Pocatello's tribe that we call *bad* Injuns. But keep in mind, boy, all these here natives march t' a different drum than we white folk, so always be on the alert when theys around."

Zeff walked across a dry field of Indian ricegrass to fetch water from the roaring Snake River. He enjoyed walking through the trees and bushes growing alongside the river. He lugged two heavy buckets of water back to Sister Woman's little campfire, then he sat down wearily. "Ah miss livin' in the woods, don't y'all, Sister Woman? Ah cain't wait till we get tuh the end o' the trail. Ah'm jus' plain ol' tired o' walkin'."

"Oh, me too, Bubba. Muh eye's ache tuh see some green growin' around us. An' muh poor ol' shoes're so worn down it's almost like walkin' barefoot. Ah surely would like tuh settle down."

Sister Woman picked up Chester Ray from his dirty, tattered quilt and propped him up over her skinny shoulder. She patted his back as she gazed around at the open plains surrounding the fort. On the far horizon, she looked at blue low rolling hills. "Ah wonder if there's any trees in those hills, Zeff."

"An' Ah'm a wonderin' if'n there might not be some clay close by. The only thing Ah knows other than huntin' an' fishin' is firin' up clay bricks."

Zeff spotted overweight old Sergeant McGraw heading to the Fort and decided to ask. He stood up on his weary legs and hustled over to catch the Sergeant before he entered the Fort. Zeff explained that he knew how to build a brick kiln to fire bricks if only he could find some clay in the area. Sergeant McGraw took him in and introduced him to the fur trader in the general store. "Mister Mackey, sir, this here be Zeff Swinton o' the Mormon handcart company camped out yonder. Mister Swinton, this is the Fort's trader, Mister Mackey."

"How're y'all doin', Mister Mackey? Nice tuh meetcha. Muh friends call me Zeff."

"Well, it's good to meet you, too, Zeff. Now, what can I be doing for you this afternoon?"

"Well suh, back in the Ozark Mountains, Ah was raised firin' clay bricks in a kiln. Ah knows how tuh build a kiln, too. So, Ah was wonderin' if'n y'all might know of any clay deposits close around the Fort. All Ah need is good clay an' Ah am in business."

"Hm. Well, a couple of years back, Chief SoYo'Cant invited me to go fishing for salmon up north of Fort Lemhi with him and his clan. The Mormons call him Chief Arimo. On the way back to the Fort, we stopped for a couple of days about five or six miles north of here on the east side of the Snake River. The womenfolk got busy cutting slender, limber willow branches and weaving them into baskets with small openings at the top. Then, they mixed some clay, exposed where the river eroded the side of a hill, with some water. They

30

smeared the wet clay over their containers, inside and out. The Chief's translator, Teniwaaten, explained to me they were making vessels to store food in. The clay sealed the jar to keep nuts and dried berries and the like away from insects and rodents, preserving the food for winter. So that's the closest clay deposit I know about. Then, later that year, I traveled south to the Portneuf River to deliver some goods the Chief had ordered. His campsite sat near a deposit of greenish clay where the Portneuf feeds into the Snake River. It's a beautiful campsite, but it's a day's ride south."

"Well, thanks, Mister Mackey. Ah thinks Ah'll mosey on up when Ah'm out huntin' this afternoon an' see if Ah can find that clay deposit up north o' here. Thanks fer the information, suh."

"Let me know what you find, Zeff. Whenever anyone digs a well around these parts, we have to pry up rough shale rocks to line it. Bricks would be a helluva lot easier to transport, stack, and build with. I'm sure you will find customers around here once the word gets out. We have a blacksmith and a cobbler to make shoes and repair saddles and bridles. We have a one-room schoolhouse and my general store and fur trading post. There's talk of a water-powered gristmill coming this way for the pioneer farmers, but I haven't yet heard of a brick maker anywhere in the territory."

Captain Hanover spread the word at the handcart camp to take a two-day rest. "Take the time t' go up t' the Fort an' replenish yer supplies fer the last leg o' the journey. Zion lies only two weeks away, due south from here, so stock up while ya can. Our next stop will be Great Salt Lake City."

Zeff borrowed a horse early that afternoon. Since he hoped to find clay, he also borrowed an empty burlap potato sack and a short-handled spade from the supply wagons. He rode west to the Snake River, then followed its meandering course north. He kept his eyes open for game and for clay. After riding for an hour and a half, he came upon a portion of the low canyon walls eroded by the river. He rode up to take a closer look. He discovered a hillside of pale gray clay. He used the small shovel to scoop up a sample and shove it into the burlap bag. When full, he tied it on behind the saddle and contin-ued on his hunt.

Zeff spotted some ducks in a narrow tributary of the broad river and switched his lead balls for buckshot. He returned to camp with six fat Mallards. The two male ducks had brilliant iridescent blue-green necks and heads, weighing about three pounds. He gave one to Sister Woman, one to Lorna Baines, and turned the other four over to the cowboys at the center of camp. Sister Woman cut up and fried the duck for their supper.

Zeff carried the small shovel and bag of clay over beside a shallow feeder creek. He mixed the clay with water and formed several bricks. He lined them up along the creek bed to dry. *I think these'll be dry enough come mornin' tuh test if the clay will be good fer firin' bricks. This's so great!*

That evening after supper, Zeff strolled over to the Baines cookfire. "Hiya, Brother an' Sister Baines."

"Good evening, Brother Swinton. Please come have a seat and join us. Thank you for the lovely duck you provided for our supper. It was delicious."

Zeff explained his wish to build a kiln and fire bricks a few miles north of the Fort alongside the Snake River. Lorna and Gilbert both sat up attentively. "This way, Ah can be close tuh hand 'ere when Connal Lee's found. They'll know here at the fort afore anyone down Salt Lake Valley way will know. Ah still believe 'e's gonna come waltzin' in any day now, sassy as ever, an' we wants tuh be on hand tuh greet 'im."

Lorna and Gilbert looked at each other in the fading light. "What do you think, dear? I miss my foster son. Should we start a farmstead here so we can be around when Connal Lee turns up?"

"Oh, I don't know. We set out for Zion, the land of milk and honey. I think we should continue our journey and see it through. I learned that the fort has weekly mail service between Fort Hall and Great Salt Lake City. Zeff could send word when Connal Lee shows up. Couldn't you, Zeff?"

Zeff nodded. "Ah suppose Mister Mackey could write y'all a note with the good news. An' should 'e turn up down in Great Salt Lake City, y'all could likewise send us word up here so's we could stop our worryin'."

"I guess that will be for the best. While out walking along the river earlier today, I was quite taken with the beauty of the plants and wildlife in the river basin. Well, Zeff, since tomorrow night will be our last night sharing the camp, perhaps you and Sister Swinton could join us for a farewell supper. We're not traveling tomorrow, so I can do up something special."

"Why, that sounds right nice, Sister Baines. Thanks. We'll be here fer sure."

"Gilbert, dear, would you please go invite that nice Captain Reed and Lieutenant Anderson to join us tomorrow night for supper? I would like to thank them personally for watching out for us on the trail. Please ask them to bring their own plates and utensils since we don't have enough for them."

"Certainly. It would be my pleasure. Good night, Brother Swinton. I'll be back right away, Lorna me darlin'."

Zeff found his raw clay bricks had set up firm and strong. *With some straw an' grass, these'll fire up jus' right.* He rushed back to share the good news with Sister Woman. They hugged with delight.

Zeff sought out Captain Hanover to let him know of their plans to stay behind and homestead north of the Fort. "Well, if yer sure, Brother Swinton. We'll miss ya an' yer wife. Thanks fer takin' such good care o' providin' fresh game fer the camp these past three months. Good luck in yer new venture."

"Thanks, Captain. Safe trails tuh y'all an' tuh all the company, too. Ah hopes we meet up again someday."

Over supper at the Baines' campfire the following evening, the Baines told their guests they had debated staying but decided to continue with the handcart company. Lorna Baines served a chocolate cake with coffee for dessert. Everyone thanked the two army officers for their guard duty on the trail.

Captain Reed replied in his Boston accent, "Why, thank you, Ma'am, for this lovely repast. I wish you and the whole company safe trails on your way south to Great Salt Lake City. I hear it's becoming quite the little town now. Those Mormons have even begun building a big stone temple."

Lieutenant Anderson stood up and extended his hand. "I would also like to thank you for inviting us to your campfire this evening,

Missus Baines. The supper was delicious. Thank you for the good company, too. Good luck with your brick kiln, Mister Swinton. I hope Connal Lee shows up soon."

The Swintons stood up to shake hands goodbye. They waved as the officers strode away to their army camp down the river a bit. Before Zeff and Sister Woman returned to their campfire and quilts, they shared tearful hugs with Lorna and Gilbert as they swore they would keep in touch, somehow. Lorna Baines kept hold of Zeff and Sister Woman's hands. "When Connal Lee turns up, we'll all get together for a big family reunion in celebration."

Early in the morning, Zeff and Sister Woman watched Captain Hanover lead the handcart company away in a southwesterly direction. "Seems strange not travelin' with 'em, don't it, Zeff?

"Yep. It sure does. Ah think Ah'm gonna miss borrowin' horses an' ammunition from the supply wagons. Now we're gonna have tuh buy a whole bunch o' stuff tuh get us all set up on our own. Come on, Sister Woman, let's push the handcart up tuh the general store an' see what they got."

While Sister Woman loaded up on flour, sugar, and salt, Zeff told Mr. Mackey of their commitment to stake a claim at the clay deposit to the north. Zeff bought gunpowder, lead for casting bullets, a shovel, and an ax, using up the last of their meager cash reserves except for three copper pennies. "An' please, Mister Mackey, we're missin' our little brover. He got separated from us several weeks back when we was attacked by those rotten, no-good Crow Injuns. He knows we were headin' here tuh Fort Hall, then on south tuh Great Salt Lake City. So, when he's able, he's gonna be comin' in along the ol' Overland Trail. He's bound tuh stop 'ere fer supplies an' news. When ya sees 'im, would ya please tell 'im we're homesteadin' up at the clay deposit? We cain't wait tuh see 'im. He's a skinny little blond boy. He's gonna turn thirteen in a coupla months. Oh, an' he's smart as a whip."

"Certainly, Zeff. I will be glad to pass along your message when I meet him. Good luck with your kiln. Come see me when you are in production."

"Will do, Mister Mackey. Thanks. Good luck tuh yew, too. So long, now."

"Goodbye, Mister Swinton. Stay safe, Missus Swinton. Welcome to the State of Deseret, otherwise known to the rest of the world as the Territory of Oregon."

As soon as they organized and loaded their purchases, Zeff and Sister Woman pushed their handcart across the open country. They headed due north with all their belongings. Six hours later, Zeff led them over to the low cliff with the clay deposit set well back from the current position of the river. The wide river basin, brimming with a variety of trees, reeds, and cattails, delighted Sister Woman. A broad expanse of flat land stretched between this side and the far ridge of the lower river plain, with the river snaking through. After walking for weeks across the barren, brown grassy plains covered with herds of buffalo and then the arid deserts of Wyoming, Zeff and Sister Woman found the Snake River bottomlands very welcoming and refreshing.

A simple man, Zeff came up with a simple plan. He would hunt for game and fish along the river for food to sell at the Fort for cash money. Sister Woman would tan the hides to trade for hard goods.

They parked the handcart, pitched their tent, and gathered smooth river rocks to line a fire pit. Hand in hand, they explored the surrounding area. Zeff carried Chester Ray in his old backpack. They walked up to the little cliff, an oversized ditch bank about ten feet tall edging the river's bottomlands. Zeff pointed to the clay deposit down the river within easy walking distance. He led Sister Woman over to where he thought they might build their little hut for wintering. They didn't have much time before the ground froze over. After gathering deadfall for their cookfire, Zeff grabbed his rifle and went hunting.

He lucked out and came upon a small herd of whitetail deer right away. He managed to down three of them before they all scattered, leaping away with the white underside of their tails raised in warning flags. One by one, he dragged the carcasses back to their camp. He hung them up, downriver, and set to butchering them. He chopped down two small Western Hemlocks the next day and dragged them over to their camp. He couldn't find any chestnut oaks as they used in the Ozarks for tanning, so he had to make do. Sister Woman knew what to do. She began carving off the bark to use its tannin. They didn't have time to dry the bark and powder it – at least not now at the start of their operation. She put the bark to boiling in her stewpot. While it stewed, she dug a deep but narrow hole in the ground. She placed the scraped and cleaned deerskins in the little pit. She poured her tannin tea, bark and all, over the pelts to cure the leather.

In the meantime, Zeff heaved the carcasses onto his handcart and laboriously hauled them to the fort. He traded the venison for a steel file to sharpen his new shovel. Then he talked Mr. Mackey into applying the balance owed for the meat to go for a deposit to buy a draft mule. In return, he promised to repay Mackey with hides as soon as they tanned them well. Smiling at his progress, Zeff jury-rigged a primitive rope harness to the handcart and hopped in. He enjoyed the luxury of traveling on wheels rather than on his own two feet, despite the jostling and bouncing from the roadless land.

Chapter 5: White Shoshone Boy

After they left the scene of the deadly encounter with the Crow warriors, Screaming Eagle, Short Rainbow, and Connal Lee rode due west. White Wolf caught up later, leading the dead warriors' horses and belongings behind him. They rode for another hour at an easy trot. Screaming Eagle called out loudly to be heard above the thundering of the horses' hooves, "I know this area. A mile or so ahead is a good place to camp by a creek. Follow me."

They trotted along, each leading a handful of horses on long lead ropes. They pulled up to a small stream and dismounted.

White Wolf went to one of the packhorses for his medicine pouches, then ordered Screaming Eagle to sit down and remove his war bonnet. He went to the stream and scooped out a gourd bowl full of clean water. As he cleaned up the bump on Screaming Eagle's head, he asked Connal Lee and Short Rainbow to unsaddle the horses. Between their seven horses and the Crow warriors' seven horses, it took them over an hour to rub down their four rides and remove all the goods and saddles from the other ten horses. Short Rainbow gestured towards the Crow supplies. "This will give us a good opportunity to make an inventory of the spoils of war. Your trophy horses are carrying a lot of valuable fur blankets and worked doeskin clothing. You won't have any trouble buying new ammunition at the trading post. You are a rich man now."

Connal Lee helped her unsaddle the horses. "But y'all should share. We all fought those danged Crow Injuns. I don't think it's fair for me to get all the horses."

Short Rainbow looked at White Wolf and twittered a bright laugh. White Wolf looked up and nodded. She answered in Shoshone, "No, no, Connal Lee. Screaming Eagle is already a rich and important man. He owns over fifty horses. White Wolf owns more than thirty. I, myself, not only own my tipi, but I have a small herd of nearly forty horses. Horses are wealth here on the plains, Connal Lee."

White Wolf finished cleaning the knot on Screaming Eagle's head. He then carefully braided the long hair that had come loose during the attack. He tied off the braid with a thin, bright red strip of deer hide. When he finished, he leaned over and gave Screaming Eagle a big hug from behind. Screaming Eagle placed his hands over White Wolf's. "Thank you, White Wolf."

White Wolf put away his medicine pouches and helped Short Rainbow prepare supper. After eating, Screaming Eagle walked over and sat down beside Connal Lee. He pulled Connal Lee up to his side so Connal Lee could lean against him. He put his strong muscled arm over Connal Lee's shoulders and gave him a warm hug. He looked up at White Wolf. "What is the English word for hero?"

Screaming Eagle lifted up Connal Lee's chin so they were looking eye to eye. "You hero. Heap big hero, Connal Lee. I adopt for be my brother."

White Wolf and Short Rainbow looked at each with a smile and a nod. "Yes, Connal Lee. We all adopt you as brother. You big hero. You our brother, now. Thank you, Connal Lee."

Connal Lee felt moved by their warm declarations that they were now family. Suddenly homesick for Zeff and Sister Woman, he turned his head into Screaming Eagle's muscled chest and cried softly. Screaming Eagle calmly rocked him and patted him on the back until he settled down. When the tears stopped, Connal Lee looked up with a hesitant smile. "Ah am happy to adopt you as my brothers and sister, too. Ah think y'all are very special, and Ah'm honored to be adopted into y'all's family."

White Wolf stepped over, knelt down beside Connal Lee, and pulled him into a hug. For the first time, he began thinking they might invite Connal Lee to join their tipi. When he let go and sat down, he spoke in Shoshone. "I predict that when Chief SoYo'Cant hears of how you rescued Screaming Eagle and saved his life, he will formally adopt you into his family and our tribe, as well."

Later in the evening, they lounged around a warm fire. Connal Lee asked in hesitant Shoshone, "Short Rainbow? You own tipi?"

Short Rainbow smiled and leaned over lovingly against Screaming Eagle's muscular chest. He pulled her into a hug. She answered in Shoshone. "Yes. We Newe are a very wise people. In our tribe, women own our homes. Everyone can own horses and dogs, but tipis are for women to own and take care of. Our job is to raise them when we make camp and take them down and load them on great horse-drawn travois when we travel between campsites. Most families have two or three wives to share the work since raising a tipi takes more than one. But I'm the only wife in our family, so far, anyway. Fortunately, I have three sisters I can ask to help when needed."

Connal Lee shook his head, bewildered. He replied in English. "Where Ah come from, the man is the head of the household. He owns the land and the house. The ladyfolk hardly never own property. They have to do the bidding of their lawfully wedded husbands."

Short Rainbow protested in Shoshone, "But, that's not civilized! To make a family, we women carefully invite a man we care for to share our tipi. If love develops and we want to make it more permanent, we declare that we are married. If we find another man or woman for whom we develop feelings of affection, we invite them to share our tipi, too. Likewise, if one of us falls out of love over time, they leave the tipi and are free to fall in love with someone else."

"Gee. That sounds so odd to me. We Americans hardly never get divorced. Even if the marriage goes bad, the husband and wife stick together for the good of their children. They might separate after the kids are grown up and go away, but not divorce. So far as I know, only rich folk in the big cities get divorces."

"I told you, Connal Lee. We Shoshone are much more civilized and wise than you Long Knives."

"Well, when y'all have children, what happens to them when y'all divorce or split up and go your own ways?"

"Usually nothing. Once a baby outgrows his moss bags and stops nursing, our parents take care of their grandchildren and teach them. Young parents are much too busy with all their daily work to take time to play with the youngsters and teach the children. The men have to hunt and protect the tribe. The women have to keep the tipi and prepare food, both for the day's meals and to preserve food for the winter. It's a lot of work. Then, we have to tan hides, sew clothing, and gather berries, nuts, grains, and fruits. We have too much to do."

White Wolf spoke up in English. "We wise people, Connal Lee. Our way best."

"Hm." Connal Lee looked around at his adopted family. "Do y'all have children?"

Screaming Eagle answered in Shoshone. "No. We keep hoping Short Rainbow will become large with child, but it has not happened yet. We three have been married just over a year now, so it should happen any time now." He tenderly pulled Short Rainbow into a closer hug. Short Rainbow nodded her head.

"How will you know who the father is, then?"

"The only important thing is to know who the mother is. Of course, Screaming Eagle and I both want to have many children with Short Rainbow. But it won't matter to us which is the father." White Wolf rose nimbly to his feet, stepped over, and sat down on the other side of Short Rainbow. He put his arm over her slender shoulders and rested his hand on Screaming Eagle's strong shoulder. He leaned over and kissed Short Rainbow on her forehead.

Short Rainbow pulled herself out of their embrace and rose gracefully to her feet. "Well, I have work to do. Let me find my store of eagle feathers, and I'll repair your war bonnet. Come, Connal Lee. While I'm sorting through our storage, I'll help you find the best of the dead Crows' fur blankets for you to sleep on tonight."

While doing their inventory, they came across a blanket sewn out of red fox furs. Connal Lee loved the soft texture and beautiful colors running in stripes. Buffalo pelts were dark brown blending into black, but these fox pelts were light tan blending into a pale reddish-brown. "Oh, I like this blanket. I think I'll keep it. Just feel how soft and smooth, Short Rainbow."

After Short Rainbow and Connal Lee walked downstream to where the horses were shackled, Screaming Eagle pulled White Wolf over to sit beside him. Screaming Eagle's muscular arm hugged White Wolf's lean shoulders. White Wolf slipped his arm around Screaming Eagle's slender waist. They smiled warmly at each other, then turned their gaze back to the fire. White Wolf rested his head against Screaming Eagle's chest, listening to his heart beating, contented with his family. "I'm sure glad those Crow warriors didn't do you more mischief. We were all worried sick last night when you didn't come back."

Connal Lee and Short Rainbow returned in time to hear that comment. Short Rainbow sat down closer to the fire and opened a leather envelope filled with eagle feathers. As she mended the bonnet, she glanced over at Screaming Eagle. "All last night, I laid wide awake worrying about you. I had a strong premonition something serious had happened. I feared they would recognize you from when you trounced their thieving war party and took back our horses. They would do more than just counting coup if they recognized you. The families of their dead warriors wouldn't have gone easy on you if they discovered you were responsible for their husbands' deaths. They would do a lot more than just stroke you."

Short Rainbow burst into tears at the thought of Screaming Eagle being tortured. She had to put down the bonnet. "I was so scared for you, Screaming Eagle. I love you so much."

Screaming Eagle scooted over and pulled her into a hug, returning her love.

In Shoshone, Connal Lee asked, "Stroke? What mean stroke?"

White Wolf answered in Shoshone. "Stroke is to gently rub the skin. However, the way Short Rainbow used the word, stroke refers to hurting a captive without drawing blood or leaving marks. They would expect the warrior to bear their tortures bravely. However, their women can become really vicious if they believe a prisoner hurt or killed their men. They would start by slicing off small pieces of their victim's body to prolong the pain and suffering as long as possible in punishment."

"Yuck! That sounds plumb awful! Why would anyone want to torture another human being? Isn't life hard enough without being intentionally mean and cruel?"

White Wolf spoke one brief word in English. "Revenge."

They fell silent as they watched Short Rainbow carefully tie new eagle fathers onto the war bonnet using horsetail hair as thread.

A few days after the rescue, their path led them across the worn-in, parallel ruts of the Overland Trail. They knew if they followed it, they would eventually arrive at Fort Hall. They rode hard, alternating between a trot at ten miles an hour and a walk at four miles an hour. A couple times a day, they dismounted and led the horses at an easy walk to give both humans and horses a break. At that pace, they averaged around sixty miles per day. Five days later, tired and dusty, they saw Fort Hall in the distance. They hadn't encountered anyone on the trail going in either direction.

White Wolf called out loudly enough to be heard over the thunder of trotting horses, "Come to Fort. I introduce Mister Mackey. He fur trader. We trade furs for weapons and supplies."

"Oh, great! Then Ah can teach y'all how to shoot, too. Ah hope he has word of Captain Hanover's handcart train. Ah can't wait to find my real family, as much as Ah love y'all, now."

They set up camp beside the Snake River. White Wolf called it the Piupa Okaipin. They all pitched in to unload the horses. They sorted what furs they wanted to keep and those they would trade at the Fort's trading post and general store. They loaded the four largest packhorses with all the skins and robes. White Wolf asked Screaming Eagle and Short Rainbow to set up camp and hunt something fresh for supper while he introduced Connal Lee to trading at the Fort.

At an easy pace, it took them half an hour before they rode their horses through the big wooden doors in the front of the Fort's stout, white plastered adobe and rock walls. They tied their six horses to a hitching post in front of the general store next to two horses with Shoshone saddles. They each pulled an armful of furs off one of the packhorses and walked through the open door of the trading post. They had to wait while the fur trader waited on an old Shoshone couple. Connal Lee watched as the trader communicated in pidgin English, pidgin Shoshone, and universal Plains Indian sign language while he traded with the old couple. To Connal Lee's pleasant surprise, he could follow the entire conversation. Finally, they struck a deal. The trader handed the Indian grandmother two small knives, twelve steel arrow heads, and a small cloth bag of bright red beads. The Indians nodded their thanks and turned towards the door.

White Wolf stepped forward. "Good morning, Mister Mackey. My name White Wolf. This my white Shoshone brother, Connal Lee. Connal Lee, this Mister Mackey. He fur trader, here."

Mister Mackey's eyebrows rose up at hearing such clear English spoken by a native boy. "Hello, White Wolf. I remember you. You came by some months ago with a big warrior. Um. Let me see now. I seem to recall his name was Screaming Eagle. Right? Hello, young man. It's good to meet you, Mister Connal Lee. You have some nice-looking pelts there. Did you come to sell them?"

"It's nice to meet you, too, Mister Mackey. Yes. Ah need gunpowder, buckshot, and lead for my double-barreled shotgun. White Wolf said y'all will trade furs for ammunition and weapons. Is that correct, suh?"

"Yes. That's right." Mr. Mackey looked sternly at White Wolf. "But just to be precise, it is against Federal law for me to trade weapons and ammunition with natives. I can trade anything else with them, but not weapons and gunpowder. Now, how many skins do you have?"

"Ah have four packhorses with big loads. Most are tanned skins. Some are already made into rugs and blankets. Ah also have quite a bit of beautifully beaded Crow Indian clothing, too."

"Well, bring everything in and lay it out on the big table over there. We'll take a look and tally up a deal."

White Wolf and Connal Lee spent ten minutes carrying in armfuls of heavy pelts. When they finished, Mr. Mackey joined them at the table. Connal Lee stood holding the yearling black bear's hide in his hands, debating if he wanted to keep it as a souvenir or not. He decided he would rather have bullets and gunpowder than a bearskin and tossed it on the pile of furs to sell. Mr. Mackey held a stub of a pencil and a small gummed pad of paper in his hands. He noted each hide and assigned a dollar value to it. When he finished his inventory, he added up what he would offer. "Well, sir. By my calculations, this cache is worth four-hundred thirty-seven dollars and twenty-five cents American. Do we have a deal?"

Connal Lee glanced over at White Wolf, his eyebrows raised in surprise and delight. White Wolf nodded his head with a big smile. "See? Short Rainbow tell you. You rich man, now, Connal Lee."

Connal Lee shook hands with Mr. Mackey to seal the deal.

"Now, Mister Lee. Do you want that in cash or in goods?"

"Well, suh, how about we shop for supplies and take any balance left over in cash at the end?"

"Sounds good. What do you young fellows want to buy?"

It took a while. They started with plenty of balls, flints, patches, gunpowder, primers, and wads. Connal Lee purchased lead bars and a mold for casting their own balls. Connal Lee then bought two Bowie knives as gifts for Screaming Eagle and Short Rainbow. White Wolf already owned a steel hunting knife. They purchased a cardboard paper packet of pins and needles along with a steel awl and thimble. They bought a cast iron frying pan with a lid. Since both Short Rainbow and White Wolf enjoyed doing beadwork, they picked out all kinds, sizes, and colors of beads. White Wolf couldn't pass up buying the last four dozen steel arrowheads with razor-sharp barbs in the store. Connal Lee became quite excited when he found a beat-up leather-bound copy of *Ivanhoe* by Sir Walter Scott. And last, they procured a small steel hatchet. White Wolf hefted the sharp axe in his right hand and observed in Shoshone, "This is small enough to be a tomahawk for war, yet large enough to fell trees."

Connal Lee responded in Shoshone, "Yes. A good weapon and a useful tool. We should buy."

Mr. Mackey watched them speaking in Shoshone with a surprised look on his face. "So, you speak Shoshone, Mister Lee? Where on earth did a young, blond white boy learn the Shoshone language?"

"Well, suh, Ah've been traveling for some weeks now with my adopted brothers, White Wolf and Screaming Eagle, and with my adopted sister, Short Rainbow. They have been good enough to teach me while we rode and at night around the campfire. It's a beautiful language, doncha know. Say, Mister Mackey, have y'all heard anything about Captain Hanover's Mormon immigrant handcart train? Ah've got family traveling with them. We got separated when some renegade Crow Indians attacked us several days this side of the continental divide. Ah got separated from them when Ah was wounded. Ah really want to find my family and let them know that Ah'm all right and still alive. Ah'm sure they are worried about me, as Ah am about them."

"Well, young man. I'm sorry to say that you missed them by a week. They headed south towards Great Salt Lake City. They should be pulling in at trails end in another five or six days if everything went right for the final leg of their journey."

Connal Lee's face fell in disappointment. He felt overwhelmed once again by a wave of homesickness. White Wolf watched and understood. He patted Connal Lee on the back, murmuring in Shoshone,

"Come on, Connal Lee. Let's go find Chief SoYo'Cant. This is the time of year he takes the clan down to Great Salt Lake City for his annual fur trading expedition. You can travel with us and be reunited with your brother and sister in a few weeks. Here. Let's get all these purchases loaded up and go back to camp for supper."

With a sad sigh, Connal Lee agreed. "Mister Mackey, do you know if Chief Arimo is still camped nearby?"

"Yes. I understand he's at his favorite campsite where the Portneuf joins the Snake River. They are camped by a small hot spring."

"Come, Connal Lee. I know just where that is. It's an easy day's ride due south of here. We'll have supper tomorrow with Uncle SoYo'Cant and all our family. Wait until I introduce you to bathing in the hot springs. Screaming Eagle just loves it. Come on. Let's get going."

"Goodbye, Mister Mackey. Thanks for all your help. Ah'll probably see you again."

"Safe travels, young man. Goodbye, White Wolf."

Chapter 6: A Day Late

For the next several days, Zeff hunted and Sister Woman tanned hides. Zeff started shoveling out a cellar space for a home to winter in.

One morning Zeff rushed down to the riverbank's edge, turned his back, and lowered his pants to go to the toilet. He unknowingly disturbed a black bear standing up to its waist in the river's currents, fishing for trout. When Zeff heard a deep bass growl behind him, he spun around and spotted a bear the height of two grown men. It started barreling towards the shore, clearly on the attack. Zeff ran for his tent as fast as he had ever run before. He hadn't been carrying his rifle. The giant bear gave chase, but the deep fast-moving water hampered it. Zeff managed to grab his rifle in time to turn and shoot the beast two times right in the face. One lead ball shot through the bear's left eye and straight into its brain. The bear collapsed dead just outside their small triangular pup tent.

Zeff and Sister Woman spent the rest of the day skinning the great beast. It took both of them to carry the thick, heavy pelt. Zeff dug the tanning hole deeper and wider to accommodate the large hide. Sister Woman boiled up tree bark tannin tea and dumped it in the tanning pit. It took three cooking pots full to fill the hole. Two days later, they had a tanned bear pelt. Zeff loaded the handcart and hooked up the mule to pull it. He walked beside the cart, transporting his furs to the Fort. He arrived ten days after Connal Lee left for Chief SoYo'Cant's winter camp.

Zeff pulled the cart up next to the door of the general store. He hefted the bearskin out and staggered into the trading post. He managed to heave the fur onto the trading table as he called out a bright and cheerful, "Howdy, there, Mister Mackey. How're y'all doin' this fine day?"

"Good afternoon, Zeff. I'm doing well, thank you. And what did you bring for me this trip?"

"Well, Ah have me a good-sized bear skin, suh, all nicely tanned up fer y'all. Plus, some other pelts an' furs, still in the cart."

"Great. Bring in your other pelts, and let's tally things up." Mr. Mackey ran his hands over the thick black fur of the black bear, native to the region. "Nice fur, Zeff. Congratulations. This will bring a pretty little penny once it's made into a rug or blanket. Now let's see what else you have."

After they finished their business, Zeff turned to leave. He stopped at the door and looked back. "Still no word from muh little brover, Mister Mackey?"

"Who?"

"Y'all knows. Ah told y'all about 'im a coupla weeks ago when we left tuh go stake our claim at the clay pit. Remember? Connal Lee?"

"Who?"

"Connal Lee."

"Now, why does that name..." After a pause, Mr. Mackey pointed an accusatory finger at Zeff. "Zeff, you told me that your younger brother was a skinny little kid and only twelve years old, didn't you?"

"Yep. Thas right."

"Well, sir, less than two weeks ago, a young man came in with one of Chief Arimo's nephews. I bought a lot of furs off him. The Indian boy, White Wolf, introduced him to me as Connal Lee. I thought Lee was his last name. But he didn't fit your description in any way."

"What duh y'all mean?"

"The young man I met stood medium height. Muscular. Neat hair. Well dressed. Clean. He was very articulate. He didn't look or speak like you at all. No offense, Zeff, but you do have a bit of a heavy southern hillbilly accent. This Mister Lee I met was very well-spoken. He even spoke passable Shoshone. Could that possibly be your little brother?"

"Yep. Sounds jus' like 'im. He went tuh school on the trail ever night. Learned tuh read an' tuh talk proper like. He's very quick on the draw, so it would be jus' like 'im tuh learn tuh speak Shoshone all in a hurry. He didn't ask about us?"

"He asked about Captain Hanover's handcart company. Come to think of it, he mentioned he had family in the company. He was very disappointed the company had departed before he arrived. He doesn't know you homesteaded here, so he must have figured you went on down to Great Salt Lake City like originally planned. I heard them talking about finding Chief Arimo and traveling with him to the Salt Lake Valley for the Chief's annual fur trading expedition. He should be pulling into Great Salt Lake City in another day or so."

"Damnation! An' here we are a waitin' fer 'im tuh show up. God damn it all!"

"I'm sorry, Zeff. I didn't put together your description of a little kid with the young man I met. I'm afraid he will expect to find you down in the Utah Territories when he arrives there. I'm sorry."

"Well, nothin' fer it, now. He'll meet up with Lorna an' Gilbert Baines. They'll tell 'im we're still up here in Fort Hall. We'll jus' have tuh wait fer 'im tuh travel back. Dang it all tuh heck an' back again!"

Zeff walked towards the door, then stopped and turned to face Mr. Mackey. "Say. Listen. Thanks fer tellin' me, Mister Mackey. Least wise, now we know he's alive an' well, an' we can stop our worryin' at last. Well, so long, Mister Mackey."

"Goodbye, Zeff. I'm sorry.

Each day Zeff spent time digging into the low cliffside. He eventually dug a hole ten feet wide and fourteen feet back from the face of the low canyon wall. He piled up the rocks he dug out near the entrance to use for building a cooking fireplace against the back wall. When the three-sided pit reached five feet deep, he stopped digging and leveled the floor. A couple of days later, he had a number of lodgepole pines chopped down and trimmed of branches. He planted four of them in the corners to support a shallowly slanted roof that rose to a peak three feet above ground level at the top of the cliff. Sister Woman moved their belongings into the rough cellar while Zeff fashioned other poles into rafters overhead. Over the next few days, between hunting, he carefully cut and notched more logs so the ends fit together where they overlapped in the corners. He tied the poles into place with wet rawhide strips, building up two-foot-high log cabin walls around three sides of their cellar home.

Zeff used their tent canvas for the front wall of their little hovel cave. They left the front open most of the time to enjoy the view of the river basin. They closed it during inclement weather. He dug up sod from the higher grounds alongside the river gully and covered the roof. Once they had a secure weather-tight hut, he notched out the back wall four feet wide and two feet deep. He then began laboriously constructing a fireplace, one heavy rock at a time. He chinked it with clay mixed with straw from the Indian rice grass growing all around them on the plains above.

Zeff hunted. Sister Woman cooked their meals and tanned hides. They worked themselves to exhaustion, preparing for the first snowfall. Over the next couple of weeks, Zeff transported more furs to Mr. Mackey and paid off the balance on his mule. From the next batch of tanned hides, he bought a couple of good steel traps. He hadn't trapped since he left his father's home in the Ozarks. Zeff caught valuable beavers, minks, raccoons, and a lynx with the new traps. Mr. Mackey paid top dollar for those hides. Zeff now had the money to buy enough flour, salt, and coffee to see them through the winter.

He finally felt secure about feeding his little family over the winter. He stopped hunting for furs so he could begin building a kiln. He invested in an expensive hand saw. He used the saw to carefully cut several lengths of pine boards. He arranged two long boards with short pieces between like a ladder. He secured the short planks to the edges using wet rawhide strips. The strips shrank as they dried, binding the mold form securely together. Next, he cut a shorter board to use as a scraper. With his sharpened Bowie knife, he whittled handles on each end of the scraper. After he mixed clay mud, he shoveled it into the mold and scraped the shorter board across, giving him uniform flat rectangular bricks.

Zeff set to work making clay mud bricks. After they cured a couple of days in the sun, he began constructing a small adobe brick kiln. He loaded up the kiln with more dried bricks and built a fire to cure the bricks in the heat. A couple weeks later, he had enough fired bricks to construct a more substantial kiln, six feet tall. After he completed the kiln, he loaded it with cured firewood, set it on fire, then sealed up the door. The next day he had charcoaled wood that would burn long and hot.

He began production of weather-resistant kiln-fired bricks. He proudly took his first cartload of bricks to the fort and told Mr. Mackey he could now start taking orders for fired bricks.

Chapter 7: Chief SoYo'Cant

Connal Lee and White Wolf carried out all the supplies they received after trading the Crow leathers and hides with Mr. Mackey. They loaded up their packhorses, then took all their new provisions back to their camp on the bank of the Snake River, south of the Fort. While they took care of business at the Fort, Screaming Eagle went hunting along the river basin and shot a small doe. When the boys arrived back at the camp, they found Short Rainbow sitting beside a small fire broiling venison steaks on a flat piece of shale heated in the red hot coals. The supplies Connal Lee had purchased delighted Short Rainbow and Screaming Eagle.

Connal Lee took great pleasure in presenting Screaming Eagle and Short Rainbow with their own Bowie hunting knives. "My way thank you for friend." They both admired the steel knives with delight. He handed them each a whetstone, pulled out his own knife, and demonstrated how to sharpen the edge. He watched while they practiced. "Keep the stones wet, now, so the knife will get real sharp."

After eating supper, they still had an hour or so of daylight. Connal Lee picked up his rifle. "Now time Short Rainbow and White Wolf practice shoot live ammunition."

Short Rainbow and White Wolf stood up, excited to practice shooting for real. Connal Lee handed the rifle to White Wolf and gave a bag of lead bullets and a bag of gunpowder to Short Rainbow. Screaming Eagle joined them to watch. They walked down to a flat, treeless meadow alongside the river. Connal Lee picked up a rock around six inches in diameter. He jogged away fifty paces and placed it on the ground. He strode back to his friends. "That will be your target today."

He invited White Wolf to load both barrels with lead bullets. "Do you remember what I showed you when you did your dry practice runs? Pull the shotgun in tight to your shoulder, sight along the barrel, and gently squeeze the trigger when you have the target in clear view."

White Wolf's first shot passed over the target and struck the ground thirty feet beyond the rock. "Remember that bullets travel flat for quite a distance before they start to fall down to the ground. You don't need to compensate by shooting higher like you do when shooting arrows. Now, try it again and aim directly for the rock."

White Wolf's second shot skimmed over the top of the target. "Load up, again. You've almost got it." White Wolf shot twice more. The lead balls struck the top of the rock both times. The rounded river run stone rolled a few feet away from the impacts. "Good job, White Wolf. Now, let Short Rainbow take a turn."

Short Rainbow took the shotgun from White Wolf, loaded both barrels, aimed, and fired. Both shots hit the target straight on, making it bounce with each impact. "Wow. You have a really good eye, Short Rainbow. Take another couple of shots, then let Screaming Eagle practice shooting." They rotated in turn, practicing until the sun had nearly set. "Good job, everyone. I think we should stop now. We don't want to waste ammunition by shooting blindly in the dark."

After a good night's sleep and a leisurely breakfast, they saddled up their horses, loaded up the pack and victory horses, and headed south. They rode parallel to the river basin, keeping the trees and shrubs on their right. Along the way, Connal Lee spotted a small herd of deer in the trees. He pulled out his double-barreled shotgun and handed it to White Wolf. "Here. Try hunting with a rifle today. Remember, the lead slugs shoot flat so aim exactly where you want to hit."

Smiling broadly, White Wolf accepted the challenge. He hopped down off his big war stallion, loaded both barrels, took aim, and fired. A doe fell to the ground. He shot again. Another doe collapsed. "Congratulations. I think you've got the hang of it now. Let's clean them using your new knives. We'll load them up on a packhorse and have gifts for Chief SoYo'Cant when we arrive at his camp."

In Shoshone, White Wolf teased Connal Lee. "You haven't even met the great Chief, and already you are trying to seek favor with him."

They cleaned the does and tied them onto the spare horses in short order. Not long after, Connal Lee spotted smoke rising ahead of them from dozens of fires. After climbing a gentle hill, they could see Chief Arimo's camp. "Gee! How many tipis are there in his camp? It looks more like a town to me with all those tipis."

White Wolf smiled, happy to be rejoining his clan. "It varies. Normally the camp has around sixty tipis and about two-hundred and fifty people. His clan owns something like eight-hundred horses and four-hundred dogs in total. Yes, it is a big encampment. Come, let's get unloaded at our family tipi. We'll take you over and introduce you to Uncle SoYo'Cant."

An hour later, they approached the center of the sprawling camp. Screaming Eagle proudly led them to an open lodge next to a tall, ornately painted tipi. The chief had built his open council chamber in a grove of young growing trees with the branches and leaves still attached. They had bound the tall, slender trees together, so their tops merged fifteen feet over head. They had covered the northern half of the living lodge with buffalo hides. Sunlight streamed in, lighting a small group of warriors and elders sitting around a smokeless hardwood fire. Chief Arimo's face lit up in a big smile when they walked up. He rose athletically to his feet and strode forward to greet them. He grabbed Screaming Eagle's broad shoulders and pulled him into a kinsman's embrace. "Welcome back, nephew."

"Thank you, Uncle SoYo'Cant. It is good to be back."

The chief turned to White Wolf and welcomed him with a big hug. Then he warmly greeted Short Rainbow as family. The middle-aged chieftain looked at Connal Lee with a puzzled look. Connal Lee respectfully removed his leather cowboy hat and held it under his left arm. White Wolf grabbed Connal Lee's arm and led him closer. "Uncle SoYo'Cant, this is our friend and adopted white brother, Connal Lee Swinton. Connal Lee, this is our great Chief SoYo'Cant. The Mormons call him Chief Arimo in English."

The Chief nodded his head. "Welcome, Mister Swinton. Please come join my fire. We talk."

Connal Lee removed his gloves and responded in Shoshone, "Thank you, Chief SoYo'Cant. I honor meet you."

They smiled at each other and shook hands. "Good. You speak Shoshone. I want all people communicate clear. Save lot trouble."

Connal Lee chuckled. "I speak little. White Wolf laugh. He say I talk like papoose. But, I learn. My good friends teach. We practice. White Wolf talk English good."

The four young people sat around the fire facing Chief SoYo'Cant. The chief, a strong athletic man in his late forties, sat straight and proud on a bear hide blanket. He wore a long-sleeved doeskin smock with long fringe hanging beneath the sleeves. The leather shirt had intricately beaded panels running along the tops of the sleeves. Over this smock, the chief wore a broad breastplate of white bone and black horn pipes proclaiming his power and position for all to see. He wore a large beaver pelt like a short cape over his shoulders for warmth. The proud chief had three large eagle wing feathers tucked into his neatly braided hair.

White Wolf told the chief the story of how they came upon Connal Lee, wounded with a Crow war arrow, lying on the ground next to a dead yearling bear cub. He described how they treated Connal Lee's wounds and how their friendship grew.

Screaming Eagle took over and told how a small group of Crow warriors had knocked him out. He described Connal Lee tracking him down early the next morning, then killing two of his attackers with his shotgun while White Wolf and Short Rainbow took care of the other three. He told the Chief he had given Connal Lee the Crow raiding party's horses, furs, and clothing as a reward for finding him so quickly and saving his life.

Chief SoYo'Cant nodded his approval. Screaming Eagle told how he had adopted Connal Lee as his brother, then White Wolf and Short Rainbow had done the same. Connal Lee had adopted them in return.

Chief SoYo'Cant nodded at Connal Lee with a slight bow from the waist. The Chief addressed him formally in Shoshone, "I thank you, Connal Lee. These three are some of my brightest and best people. They are all smart, talented, and hard-working. They work so well as a team I would hate to see them split up. Thank you for saving the life of my apprentice War Chief, Screaming Eagle."

Connal Lee responded in Shoshone, "White Wolf and Short Rainbow medicine save my life. Glad do same. They special family. All good friend, now."

White Wolf stood up and signed for Screaming Eagle to join him. They left Connal Lee to become acquainted with the tribe's Chief. They returned half an hour later with two heavy, cleaned, and skinned does. They showed the venison to Chief SoYo'Cant. "Connal Lee has been teaching us to shoot a rifle. I hunted with his double-barreled shotgun this morning and shot these two does. They are for your supper tonight, Uncle SoYo'Cant, with our thanks for your kind welcome back to your camp."

White Wolf and Screaming Eagle set the does down close to the cookfire on the east side of the big tipi beside the lodge. The chief's middle-aged first wife stepped out of the tipi. She had neatly braided her graying hair into two waist-long braids. A preteen girl and a teenage girl followed her out of the tipi. They all greeted each other affectionately as close family. White Wolf introduced Connal Lee to the chief's first wife, White Dove, their beloved aunt.

With a fast spate of orders, she instructed the two girls to roll both heavy carcasses onto old hides and drag them downstream to butcher for their supper. Giggling, the girls followed her orders. White Dove followed along to supervise. She waved back to the group around the fire as she sauntered away. Several of the family's dogs smelled the raw meat and followed the young girls most attentively, barking in excitement. The large tan dogs had black tips on their fur and white legs and underbellies. Their large ears stood up erect and alert as they began salivating.

Chief SoYo'Cant introduced his language teacher and translator, Teniwaaten. Teniwaaten stepped over to Connal Lee to shake his hand. Connal Lee stood up and removed his hat again. While they shook hands, Teniwaaten said in clear English, "If you need help with a word, my tipi is always open to you. Please come visit me if you would like to practice your Shoshone."

"Why, thanks so much, Teniwaaten. That's mighty neighborly of y'all. Yer tribe is certainly a friendly group of people, unlike some of the stories I have heard about other tribes."

Before Connal Lee and his adopted family left to prepare their own supper, Chief SoYo'Cant shook his finger at Connal Lee. "Other tribes, like Chief Pocatello's saididig teach their papooses it is honorable to kill other tribes, including Long Knives of the white man tribe, when they intrude on our hunting grounds. Be careful not to leave the camp unless Screaming Eagle or White Wolf accompany you. They will keep you safe. Pocatello may be Shoshone with a good Bannock wife, but he does not believe in peaceful co-existence with our white neighbors as I do. He is always advocating war with the white man. He would not be kind if he found you alone."

Connal Lee responded in Shoshone. "Thank you for warn. I stay with friends all time." He then turned to White Wolf and whispered, "What mean saididig?"

"Dog Stealers. I explain later."

That evening after Connal Lee and his spouses finished supper, Connal Lee lay down with his head in White Wolf's lap. He patted his stomach, a satisfied smile on his face. "White Wolf? It seems to me that all the Indians I have seen up close are taller, stronger, and more muscular than the average Americans or Europeans. Healthier. Have you ever noticed that? I wonder why?"

"Because we wise people. We eat good food, work hard, build muscle. Build strong. For Shoshone, wealth no gold. Wealth able feed all people all time. Only time one hungry is if all hungry. Children grow strong on good food from young age. White man small from child of poor food. Plus, white man sick all time. We healthy all time. No sick until Long Knives brought um sick to our camps."

"What? You mean the Indians didn't have illness or disease until the white man came?"

"That right. First big sick nineteen winters ago. Before Mormon come. Smallpox winter. Every tribe, far and near, all sick smallpox. We call it rotting face disease winter. Everyone sick. Bad sick. One of three die. Whole clans die. Empty tipis. Empty wigwams. Empty villages. Mostly wise elders and leaders die. Young no bad sick. Smallpox scar face, hands, body. We handsome people. Vain of beauty. Ashamed scar not battle wound. Many scarred so bad prefer no live ugly. More old die. Who teach children? Who work? Who hunt? Who cook? Bad, bad time."

The little family sat quietly, solemn after such a serious turn of conversation. White Wolf patted Connal Lee's shoulder, then switched to speaking Shoshone. "Now, every winter is a winter of sickness. Long Knives have been traveling through our hunting grounds on the Overland Trail more and more in the past ten winters. Mormon settlers and adventurers headed to the California gold rush pass through our lands. Every winter, we suffer more influenza, colds, and whooping cough. Sometimes even cholera, which always takes a heavy toll among our proud people. Every winter, we lose more and more people to white man diseases."

Connal Lee nodded his head sadly. "I had cholera back on the Great Plains when we were camped across the river from Scotts Bluff. Almost everyone in the camp came down with it. Some real bad, some not so sick. We lost a lot of our people that week. One in ten didn't survive."

"All disease is bad, but more so for Indians. Our medicines do not help with white man diseases. No ritual or herb can cure the diseases spread by white travelers. When we take sick, we are all afraid we might die. When the plague, diphtheria, typhus, or tuberculosis strike our camps, we all become afraid for each other and for ourselves."

"I'm sorry, White Wolf."

"Don't be, Connal Lee. It's not your fault."

For the next few days, Connal Lee accompanied his three friends as they visited with their friends and family. He spent more time listening to the council surrounding Chief SoYo'Cant. He practiced conversation with Teniwaaten, both in English and in Shoshone. He came to respect the English teacher's logical way of teaching Shoshone. Under Teniwaaten's tutelage, Connal Lee began conjugating verbs. He stopped talking baby talk, all in the present tense, after he learned the past and future tenses of the most common verbs.

Each day more of the clan arrived, assembling to travel en masse to Salt Lake Valley. The camp grew in numbers but not in tipis. The new arrivals didn't raise their tipis for such a short stay.

One day, after eating a simple breakfast with hot sage tea, White Wolf invited Connal Lee to accompany him to visit his respected teacher, Chief SoYo'Cant's most valued medicine man, Firewalker. Firewalker, a venerable old gentleman, wore his white-gray hair in simple long braids bound up in furs, feathers, and beads. He wore the weapons of a warrior and the jewelry of a woman. At White Wolf's request, Connal Lee allowed Firewalker to inspect his scars from the Crow arrow and the bear attack. Firewalker complimented White Wolf on his treatments. They spent most of the day discussing skin infections from dirty claws and how to treat them. Connal Lee didn't follow all the conversation since they used many unfamiliar words not used in everyday life.

As they walked back to Short Rainbow's tipi, White Wolf explained how Firewalker and he were shamans. "But since we focus on the physical body and treatments using herbs and medicines more than rituals, white men called us medicine men. We study all the lore, stories, and rituals, the same as Short Rainbow and Burning Fire. But we concentrate more on the gifts of mother earth rather than spiritual gifts."

As they finished supper, White Wolf suggested they visit the little hot spring over by the river. Screaming Eagle's face lit up at the idea. He sprang to his feet, then reached down to help Short Rainbow stand up. White Wolf held his hand out to Connal Lee. "Come."

Connal Lee followed his Shoshone friends as they headed towards the Tobitapa River, west of the big camp. Screaming Eagle enthusiastically led the way at a quick pace. About ten minutes later, they entered a cluster of small trees. White Wolf stopped Connal Lee. "Watch your step. The river bank is pretty steep right here. Some of the rocks are loose, so don't trust your footing."

Connal Lee heard water running in the six-foot-wide creek, a small tributary of the Portneuf River. The fast-flowing water had eroded the soil over the years, exposing rocks large and small along both banks. The sun had set, leaving them in a calm twilight. Connal Lee saw wisps of steam floating along the bottom of the river bed in the cool dry air.

When they reached the little hot spring bubbling out of the side of the riverbank, Screaming Eagle began pulling off his clothes as fast as he could. Connal Lee watched them disrobe and toss their clothing up on the higher bank and decided to join them. They splashed into the little pool of water edged by rocks where the hot water mixed with the creek's cold water. When Connal Lee saw his friends' smiles as they floated in the shallow hot water, he lunged right in, splashing water playfully. They all laughed and began splashing each other. When they calmed down, Screaming Eagle pulled Connal Lee over closer to the little creek. They sat down on an underwater ledge, a natural bench in the side of the pool. Their shoulders and necks rose above the steaming bath. Screaming Eagle scooted over close to Connal Lee, put his arm around Connal Lee, and hugged him. "Good."

Connal Lee snuggled up closer. "Real good."

Screaming Eagle murmured in Shoshone, "Relax now. Let the heat soak into your muscles while the water washes us clean. I just love hot water. Don't you?"

Short Rainbow pulled her braids undone. She leaned over and washed her crinkled black hair in the running water. When she finished, she snuggled up to Connal Lee's other side. White Wolf sat down beside her. They all cuddled affectionately, enjoying the warmth. Connal Lee leaned over Short Rainbow to look at White Wolf. "Where does the hot water come from?"

White Wolf answered in Shoshone, "I have never heard an explanation or reason for it. It's just another gift from mother earth. On our way to Great Salt Lake City, we will pass an area with many hot springs bubbling up out of the earth. Like so many of nature's abundant gifts, though, not all hot springs are benevolent. Many days ride north of here in the great mountains where we hunt in the summer, in an area the explorers and fur trappers named Teton Peaks, you will find hundreds of hot springs. Some even shoot water up into the air to great heights. Some are so hot they are dangerous to life, hot enough to cook food. Many smell like rotten eggs, while others flow clear and sweet as snowmelt."

Connal Lee snuggled up contentedly, relaxing from the heat penetrating his muscles. "Hm."

Screaming Eagle's free hand lapped hot water up over his face and shoulders, a look of bliss on his face. He hadn't removed his silver armbands below his bulging biceps. Short Rainbow jumped, then twittered a happy laugh as she pushed White Wolf's hand away from her exposed crotch. White Wolf grabbed at her again, playfully. She rolled over Connal Lee's body and sat in Screaming Eagle's lap. "Protect me, Screaming Eagle. I'm under attack."

They all chuckled. A few minutes later, Short Rainbow felt Screaming Eagle's erection rubbing against her backside. She turned around and carefully lowered herself over his crotch. After completing the connection, she snuggled up against Screaming Eagle's brawny chest, kissing and licking his muscular neck. Connal Lee felt them undulating beside him. When he realized they were making love, his penis grew fully erect. White Wolf pulled himself closer to Connal Lee. He reached over and took hold of Connal Lee's manhood with his right hand. With his left, he picked up Connal Lee's left hand under the water and placed it on his own erection. He began gently massaging Connal Lee, leisurely pulling his foreskin up and back down. Connal Lee sighed and let his head fall over to rest on White Wolf's shoulder. They smiled at each other. Connal Lee felt Screaming Eagle and Short Rainbow's exercises become more athletic with lots of sighing and mumbled endearments. White Wolf leaned across Connal Lee's squirming torso, picked up Short Rainbow's long wet hair, and nuzzled her neck, kissing and licking behind her ear. It didn't take long for Connal Lee to melt beneath White Wolf's hand and slick wet torso. He released his orgasm with a loud moan of pleasure as his toes curled in ecstasy. White Wolf happily followed moments later. They collapsed back with their arms around each other's shoulders. They watched Short Rainbow bouncing on Screaming Eagle's lap, encouraged by his enthusiastic pelvic thrusts. Finally, Short Rainbow and Screaming Eagle soared to heaven with long sighs and moans. When they quieted down, the four sat side by side with contented smiles.

Connal Lee thought back to some eight months past, the last time his father had forcibly penetrated his mouth and butt, sadistically tormenting his young son to achieve his own selfish sexual gratification. *Wow. What a difference. Paw always hurt me. He always stank. His breath stank of moonshine and tobacco. When he finished using my body, he always pushed me away like something foul and insignificant. What a difference. My adopted Indian brothers and sister smell wonderful, like clean earth, fresh air, cold water, and hardwood smoke. Their touches feel gentle and caring. They share their pleasure with each other, paying attention to the others' delight before taking their own. Oh, Ah think Ah'm going to like growing up. Wouldn't it be nice if they fell in love with me? Ah would love to have someone to love. Ah think Ah'm starting to fall in love with all three of them.*

Connal Lee impetuously leaned over and kissed Screaming Eagle's cheek. Then he kissed Short Rainbow's cheek. Turning his head, he then kissed White Wolf's cheek. They smiled at each other. White Wolf kissed him back on his lips with a playful little lick.

Short Rainbow stood up and began stripping the water from her hair. "Let's go back while there's still enough light to see the way."

The boys nodded their agreement. They all stood up and began stripping the water off each other's bodies. They scampered up out of the five-foot-deep creek bed into a cold breeze on the higher land. They pulled on their clothing as fast as they could. Short Rainbow shuddered at the shocking temperature change. Screaming Eagle pulled her into his arms to help her warm back up, then helped her pull on her clothing. White Wolf led the way back to where they could see campfires burning in the camp. Screaming Eagle held Short Rainbow's hand. Connal Lee reached out and took her free hand in his, then found White Wolf's hand. They walked along slowly, carefully finding their way as darkness descended around their happy group of loving friends.

The morning after bathing in the hot springs, Connal Lee met the renowned shaman, Burning Fire, Short Rainbow's tutor. Short Rainbow explained how Burning Fire could leave her body and enter the supernatural world to search for answers to the tribe's problems. Everyone respected her and valued her as a prophetess. The tribe visited her to heal sickness caused by evil spirits, like nightmares, depression, and anxieties. Even though in her forties, Burning Fire maintained the lean and lithe body of a younger woman. She reminded Connal Lee of an older version of Short Rainbow, intelligent, athletic, and graceful.

That afternoon, SoYo'Cant's oldest son, Arimo, arrived with his slender young Ute wife. They had been traveling and hunting with another clan of Shoshones to the north in the Grand Teton mountains. They came carrying plenty of dried meats, fish, and berries to augment their hunting during the lean winter months. While the wives of his clan set up their temporary camps, Arimo rushed over and greeted his cousins. Born the same month, Arimo and White Wolf's parents had raised them like brothers. They loved each other like brothers and best friends. After White Wolf introduced him to Connal Lee, Arimo invited everyone to accompany him to report to his father.

Chief SoYo'Cant greeted his namesake with a great show of warmth. The chief invited everyone to join him around his campfire. "At last, our clan has assembled. Tomorrow we leave for the valley of the great bad waters lake. This land cannot sustain so large a gathering for long in one place. We leave at first light."

In the dawn's early twilight, Short Rainbow enlisted her sisters to help dismantle her tipi. They packed the heavy buffalo hides on four great travoises strapped onto the shoulders of her largest and strongest packhorses. They loaded their other belongings and food supplies on three more travoises.

Chief Arimo's trade journey departed the Portneuf River as the sun peaked above the hills. Over a thousand men, women, and children made up the chief's clan making the trip. They carried all their belongings with them. The great clan rode and herded over five-thousand horses along with their company. All but the very youngest children knew how to ride. Their nomadic tribe taught their young how to ride first thing. By the time their children could walk, they felt comfortable on horseback. The travelers carried their infants in moss bags on their mothers' backs or strapped onto one of the families' travois. It appeared to Connal Lee that nearly as many large dogs accompanied the group as horses. He had never seen so many dogs before.

They stopped the second night of the journey to camp alongside several gushing hot springs. The entire gathering enjoyed resting in the flowing hot waters of the springs.

Chief SoYo'Cant invited Screaming Eagle's family and Connal Lee to eat supper with him. When they walked towards the Chief's campfire, they passed several cookfires attended by the Chief's wives, daughters, and nieces. They stopped briefly to pay their respects to the Chief's first wife, White Dove.

When they approached the Chief's fire, they found a large group of men sitting in two concentric rings around a large fire. The Chief's oldest and most respected councilors and advisors sat in the inner ring. In the outer ring sat the heads of influential families and the leaders of the clan's warriors. The chief stood up and waved for them to sit near him. He invited Connal Lee to take a seat on his right in the place of honor. Teniwaaten sat on Connal Lee's other side to translate if needed. Connal Lee looked a question at White Wolf, but White Wolf merely shrugged that he didn't know. As they sat down, young girls arrived carrying drinking horns of red tea made from dried service-berry leaves.

Chief SoYo'Cant stood. The group fell silent, all eyes on their leader. The chief spoke in a loud oratorical voice. "This young boy, Connal Lee Swinton, has done a great service for our tribe. He saved Screaming Eagle from torture and likely from death at the hands of our hated enemies, the dishonorable Crow. Crow warriors captured Screaming Eagle with a cowardly attack from behind. In repayment of Connal Lee's bravery and tracking skills and in repayment of his saving the life of my beloved nephew and apprentice War Chief, I now formally adopt Connal Lee as my son. Spread the word among all the clans of the tribe and all the neighboring tribes that Connal Lee is now my son, my family. If anyone does him ill or harm, they will answer to me for an attack on my family. Connal Lee, please stand up."

Connal Lee rose athletically to his feet and gazed into the chief's warm brown eyes. "Connal Lee, you are now my son from this mo-ment on. You may come to me with any problem or to ask for any help you require. I require my sons to honor our family and tribe and obey our laws. Will you accept my adoption and become my son?"

Connal Lee nodded his head yes. Screaming Eagle, White Wolf, and Short Rainbow moved to stand behind Connal Lee in a show of support and approval. Connal Lee answered in Shoshone. "Yes, great Chief SoYo'Cant. I much honor be son." The chief stepped forward, put his hands on Connal Lee's shoulders, and pulled him into a gentle kinsman's embrace. He patted Connal Lee three times on the back, then pulled away and gave him a nod. Screaming Eagle turned Connal Lee around and hugged him. "Welcome, cousin. You are no longer our adopted brother. You are now our formally adopted cousin."

White Wolf pulled Connal Lee out of Screaming Eagle's arms and embraced him. "I told you our great Chief would probably adopt you in reward for saving Screaming Eagle's life. Now you are truly one of us."

Not to be left out, Short Rainbow pushed her way between the two boys and drew Connal Lee into a big hug. "I'm so happy for you, Connal Lee. Now we are all family."

Connal Lee didn't know the Shoshone words to express his joy, but his huge smile said it all. He turned and nodded formally to the Chief. "Thank you, Chief SoYo'Cant. Much honor. Happy. Thank you."

Everyone resumed their seats. The women and girls began serving supper to celebrate the formal adoption of Connal Lee into the Shoshone Tribe. After everyone finished eating the delicious feast, the chief indicated two of his warriors sitting in the outer circle. They both stood up and removed long peace pipes from intricately beaded tubes of doeskin. They set down the carrying cases, then filled the pipes with tobacco and other herbs from small leather pouches. The warriors carried the pipes to their Chieftain.

"Connal Lee, please rise. Now we smoke the peace pipe to seal your adoption to me, my family, and our great Shoshone nation, the Newe. Will you smoke the peace pipe with me, my son?"

Connal Lee had never smoked before. Even though afraid of doing it wrong, he nodded. "Yes, Chief SoYo'Cant. I honor smoke peace pipe with you."

Two young girls walked up with burning twig matches and lit the pipes. The warriors held out the pipes with both arms and bowed to the chief. Chief SoYo'Cant picked up one of the peace pipes and turned to face the west. He raised up the pipe and bowed slightly. He puffed the pipe before allowing the smoke to escape from his mouth. He saluted the north and took another puff of smoke. Again, he turned to the east and repeated the ceremonial gestures. Solemnly he turned south, raised the pipe with a bow, and puffed a fourth time. He softly touched the pipe to the ground, smoked it, then raised it overhead to salute the Great Spirit with another small toke. After the smoke seeped from his mouth, he handed the pipe to Connal Lee with a bit of a bow. Connal Lee bowed in return when he accepted the burning pipe. He hesitantly pulled a little smoke in his mouth but didn't inhale it, afraid he would cough and disturb the occasion's solemnity. As the smoke drifted out of his mouth, he looked a question at the chief. His newly adopted father gestured to pass the pipe to Teniwaaten, sitting on his other side. The chieftain then took the second pipe, toked it, and handed it off to Arimo, sitting on his left. Connal Lee sat down when the chief sat back down, proud he hadn't coughed. Teniwaaten slapped his back. "Congratulations, cousin. Welcome to the Shoshone Nation."

Half an hour later, after everyone had a turn at the peace pipes, the assembly disbanded. Screaming Eagle, White Wolf, and Short Rainbow surrounded Connal Lee to accompany him back to their family cookfire. They spread out their sleeping furs and snuggled up for warmth as the night cooled down. They spoke quietly as they watched the fire burn low. Connal Lee slept that night wrapped in Screaming Eagle's strong warm arms. Short Rainbow slept in Connal Lee's arms with White Wolf snuggled up on her other side. White Wolf happily stretched his arm over his beloved family and newly adopted cousin. His hand rested on Screaming Eagle's bulging bicep, just above his silver armband. Not for the first time, White Wolf considered what it would mean to their family if they invited Connal Lee to share their tipi.

Chapter 8: Great Salt Lake City

The clan's horses with travoises, riders, packsaddles, or running unburdened in the herd spread out along a two-mile course. They traveled due south at a leisurely walking pace of around three miles an hour. A couple of days after leaving the hot springs, they arrived in a beautiful valley surrounded on all sides by gentle foothills. A creek flowing south from the Bear River Mountains watered the flat valley. In a couple of years, Brigham Young would call several families of settlers on life missions to move to the valley and begin farming it. They would name their little town Logan after Ephraim Logan, an early fur trapper in the area who left his name on the Logan River. The great range of the snow-capped Wasatch Mountains rose to the east, looming over the foothills.

While they traveled, Chief SoYo'Cant invited Connal Lee and Arimo to sit in on his tribal councils in the early evenings. After they concluded discussions of tribal affairs, Connal Lee sometimes stayed and ate supper with the Chief. They conversed on many subjects in both English and Shoshone. Connal Lee told his adopted father how he desired to find his older brother and sister, Zeff and Sister Woman. "Only four more day we reach Great Salt Lake City, Connal Lee. There we find you family."

"Oh, thank you, Father SoYo'Cant. I can't wait to see them and let them know that I am alive and doing well."

"Patient. We get there."

Some evenings, Connal Lee spent his time studying with Teniwaaten. His Shoshone vocabulary and grammar improved dramatically with the intensive tutoring.

Connal Lee cherished the night when he could snuggle up to his loving friends, his adopted cousins, under their sleeping furs. Sometimes the Shoshone spouses drew him into their love play. Sometimes he took the initiative and pushed his way into their lovemaking. He learned to be selfless in affectionate playfulness, paying attention to the needs and wishes of his partners before his own. He did his best to give pleasure equally to all three spouses. They, in turn, always made sure Connal Lee reached a climax by the conclusion of their love play.

The clan's path took them close to the shores of the enormous Great Salt Lake, a body of water so vast Connal Lee couldn't see the distant shore. He tasted the water and discovered the lake truly deserved the Indian name of Bad Waters Lake. The wives of the camp scooped up dried salt from shallow ponds evaporating along the lake's sandy white shore to flavor their food. Connal Lee wondered how they would separate the salt from the sand.

Finally, their journey took them past the young orchards and unfinished adobe fort of Bountiful, a few miles north of Great Salt Lake City. White Wolf told Connal Lee they would camp that night outside the adobe city walls of the massive city. To their west rose a beautiful mountain, an island in the lake. To their east rose craggy, snow-covered mountains the French fur traders had named The Rocky Mountains over a hundred years ago.

Midafternoon, Chief SoYo'Cant led his tribe to the campground they had used before, due west of one of the gates in the ten-foot-high adobe and rock wall nearly surrounding the territorial capital. Even though the Mormons had built only six miles of the fortification out of the much larger project, it still presented a massive and impressive undertaking. The wives and daughters of the clan raised their tipis, settling in for a stay of a week or more. Chief SoYo'Cant invited Connal Lee, Screaming Eagle, and White Wolf to accompany him into the city. "I introduce heap big chief Mormon Tribe, Brigham Young. He maybe know where find family, Connal Lee."

"Oh, thank you, Father SoYo'Cant. Aeshen." The three Shoshones rode their great warhorses through the gate. Connal Lee rode his pretty, dark brown mare. Screaming Eagle had visited Brigham Young with his uncle in past years. He led the way, proudly wearing his war bonnet. The fine homes they passed with flower gardens and young trees in front impressed Connal Lee. All the houses had vegetable and herb gardens, barns, sheds, and carriage houses in their back yards. They rode past a few old log cabin houses, the remaining few of the first homes put up in the valley ten years ago when the Mormons first arrived. Most had been replaced with larger adobe and wood board homes.

Great snowcapped mountains of the Wasatch Range defined the eastern edge of the fortified city. They could see the flat shores of Great Salt Lake to the west, quite a distance away. The great Jordan River and other smaller creeks brought water to the fields and gardens of the large town. Away from the rivers and irrigated land, arid desert made up the landscape for as far as the eye could see.

When Brigham Young first arrived in 1847, he ordered the city be laid out in the plan revealed by Joseph Smith for the holy city of Zion. The church surveyors laid out a plat one-mile square designed to accommodate fifteen thousand Mormons and their temples, storehouses, schools, and chapels. Within the plat, Brigham Young ordered a grid of ten-acre squares 660 feet to a side, separated by streets 132 feet wide. Brigham Young told his surveyors, "The streets shall be wide enough for a covered wagon and a team of four oxen to turn around without resorting to profanity."

According to Joseph Smith's plan, they divided each square into half-acre lots, 66 feet by 330 feet. They set aside the land surrounding the compact residential blocks for agriculture and animal husbandry within close travel distance. Joseph Smith's celestial plan of Zion specified that each lot contain a single home built back 25 feet from the street to allow for a garden and a grove of trees in the front yard.

Screaming Eagle led their small party east along a broad avenue named Brigham Street. Connal Lee gazed all around, amazed at the gracious adobe and wood homes. The adobe brick walls, plastered with gray clay, looked like gray cut stone masonry. Brigham Street would soon be renamed South Temple. When they rode past the fifteen-foot-tall stone wall surrounding Temple Square, the chief and Screaming Eagle discussed how it had changed from last year. The Mormon Church had begun building the foundation of a great granite temple four years earlier. Now Temple Square looked like a freshly plowed field with no sign of the foundation.

When they arrived at the stately governor's mansion, they dismounted and tied up their horses to the sidewalk's hitching posts. Six-foot-tall granite obelisks with heavy chains swagged between them formed the hitching rails. A gracious mansion with a beehive sculpture on its rooftop stood on their right. Connal Lee glanced to the left and found two smaller buildings, then a narrow two-story home with a statue of a lion lounging above its door. Screaming Eagle and Chief SoYo'Cant removed their feathered war bonnets and tied them onto their saddles.

White Wolf leaned in and confided to Connal Lee that Chief Brigham Young had forty-seven wives and several dozen children. Many of his wives lived either in Beehive House or in the new Lion House next door with twenty bedrooms on the second floor. Connal Lee's eyes grew wide in astonishment. He leaned in close to White Wolf and whispered, "Forty-seven wives? For real?"

Screaming Eagle led the way up the short pathway and knocked on the heavy wooden door between massive bastions in the eight-foot-tall stone wall. The wall had been built to protect the Brigham Young Estate by the same Scandinavian craftsmen who had constructed the wall around the city.

A few moments later, a middle-aged, nicely dressed woman opened the gate. She smiled when she recognized the callers and invited them in. She led them up the path onto the porch spanning the width of the three-story mansion. She opened the double doors and beckoned them to enter. The gracious Victorian appointments and furnishings inside the home impressed Connal Lee. He had no idea people lived in such beautiful homes. The lady gestured to a spacious room to her right. "Kindly wait in the parlor while I let the Governor know you have arrived."

A few moments later, the woman led them back through the foyer to Brigham Young's office opposite the parlor. She tapped on the door and then opened it to announce Chief Arimo. Brigham Young stood up behind his desk and invited them to enter. He stepped over and held out his hand to Chief SoYo'Cant. After they shook hands, he indicated the two leather armchairs in front of a small fireplace. "Please have a seat, Chief Arimo."

Chief SoYo'Cant pointed at Screaming Eagle before he sat down. "Nephew. Apprentice War Chief. Screaming Eagle."

Brigham Young nodded. "Yes. I remember you, Screaming Eagle. Welcome. I also remember you, White Wolf. You are very welcome, as well. Peace."

Connal Lee glanced curiously around the office. A nicely dressed man sat at a small writing desk in the corner, scribbling away in a journal. The desk held a large hutch on its top with open slots holding books and two closed doors. Connal Lee examined Brigham Young, a clean-shaven fifty-seven-year-old man, as he shook Screaming Eagle and White Wolf's hands. The smiling leader of the Mormons wore his hair trimmed to the bottom of his ears, parted on the right, and combed back off his broad forehead in a wave. He sported two gold watch chains over a black silk vest. A Freemason pin showed prominently on his white shirt below a floppy black silk bowtie. He stood a couple of inches taller than Connal Lee's five foot eight inches. The big-boned man had a barrel-shaped torso and weighed around two-hundred pounds.

The Chief gestured towards Connal Lee. "This adopted white Shoshone son, Connal Lee Swinton. He want find family."

Connal Lee took that as his cue. He stepped up and shook hands with the Territorial Governor and President of the Mormon Church. "A pleasure to meet y'all, suh. My family and I were traveling with Captain Hanover's immigrant handcart company. A couple of weeks west of the continental divide, a Crow war party attacked us. Ah was out hunting away from the company when they shot me." With a warm smile, he nodded at White Wolf. "White Wolf here saved my life. He's studying to be a medicine man shaman. The fur trader at Fort Hall told me the handcart company came on down to Great Salt Lake City. They should have arrived a couple of weeks ago. Do y'all have any news of them?"

Brigham Young sat down behind his broad desk. "Why, yes, young man, I do. Bishop Hanover disbanded his company here in Great Salt Lake City and then reported to me on his journey. He said some of his company liked the looks of the small farming community of Bountiful, so they wanted to farmstead there. Others returned north to Fort Farmington to establish their homesteads. I believe he said most of them accepted his invitation to continue on south to Fort Utah. The Bishop operates a farm and cattle range just south of the little township of Fort Utah in Provo. They are located on Hobble Creek. It's beautiful country down there with abundant water. It's another forty-five miles away to the south, around the bend of the mountain range."

"Oh. Thanks very much, suh. My brother is Zefford Ray Swinton. My sister goes by Sister Woman. They have a little boy, Chester Ray. Have y'all heard anything about them?"

Brigham Young, who had a good memory for names and faces, thought a moment, then shook his head. "Sorry. I don't believe I've had the pleasure of meeting them. But, we're a growing city. We have nearly twenty thousand Saints living just in this valley alone and forty-thousand Mormons in the Territory."

Connal Lee felt another pang of disappointment. "Could y'all please tell me how Ah might go about tracking down my family, suh?"

"If they settled here in the valley, I'm sure they introduced themselves at one of the stores or shops. Many pioneers leave word of where they intend to settle at the post office. That way, if any mail arrives care of general delivery, the postmaster knows where to forward it to. If you can't find word of them, I would advise you to travel down to Fort Utah and look up the good bishop. Everyone knows him down there, so you won't have any trouble finding him."

"Well, thanks anyway, Governor. It's been an honor to meet y'all, suh."

White Wolf put his hand on Connal Lee's shoulder. "I know the way to Provo. If we need to go there to find your family, I will be happy to guide you."

"Thanks, White Wolf. Aeshen."

Before they left Brigham Young's office, Chief SoYo'Cant asked White Wolf to translate for him. Through White Wolf, he sought to know why the Mormons had stopped construction on the new temple in Temple Square. Brigham Young scowled. "Well, Chief Arimo, that rascal, the new President of the United States of America, has dispatched two-thousand five-hundred army foot soldiers to put down polygamy by force of arms if necessary. Mister Buchanan ran on a campaign denouncing plural marriage and slavery. After the election, he evidently decided to act against polygamy and the Mormon Church as he had promised during his campaign. I suppose he figured we were an easier objective than taking on slavery and all the southern states. We received word on July the twenty-fourth, the tenth anniversary to the very day of when we first arrived in this great valley. I mobilized the Nauvoo Legion, and we began preparing for war. We also began preparations to abandon our northern settlements and burn our crops and homes. We will not surrender our homes to Colonel Johnston's men nor let them enjoy any of the fruits of our labors. We have armed every male between six and sixty, preparing for the worst. I presently have fifteen hundred men building defensive breastworks and rifle pits in Echo Canyon and East Canyon to defend the main roadways of the Mormon Trail into Great Salt Lake Valley from the east. In a nutshell, we buried the temple's foundation to protect it until we can resume construction in times of peace."

While White Wolf translated, Chief SoYo'Cant leapt to his feet, alarmed and disturbed at the idea of twenty-five hundred armed troops entering his tribe's traditional hunting grounds. He knew it would inflame the war hawks like Chief Pocatello. It would lead to even more attacks on whites and Mormons when word got out. White Wolf translated the chief's concerns. The chieftain asked if Brigham Young had sent a warning to his son's friend, Andrew Hayes, serving a mission in Fort Lemhi.

"Yes, Chief. I dispatched messengers to the Fort a couple months ago when this all started. Chief Arimo, my old friend, the Shoshones have been friends and allies to the Mormons since we first arrived. Perhaps you and your military leaders and councilors could join me tomorrow morning for a council of war. I will order the officers of the Nauvoo Legion to attend to brief us on the strategies we have worked out. I believe you deserve to know our plans. I would like to hear your evaluations and recommendations. This is your land coming under attack, too."

They listened to Chief SoYo'Cant's deliberations, then White Wolf translated his words for Brigham Young. "Great Chief Mormon Tribe, Chief Arimo thank you for invite to war council. Chief Arimo say he want bring war chief, family, two elder councilors of great wisdom, and translator. Ten in total. You agree?"

"Yes, certainly." Brigham Young scribbled himself a note. "I will prepare for your ten men plus what officers I can round up this afternoon. Let's all meet here at Beehive House two hours after dawn."

White Wolf translated, then agreed on Chief SoYo'Cant's behalf.

Brigham Young walked over and shook hands, adjourning their meeting. "I only hope we can delay the army without loss of blood on either side."

After leaving Beehive House, his Shoshone family accompanied Connal Lee in searching for his two white families. They visited the general store, trading post, dry goods store, and post office. No one had heard anything about the Swintons or the Baines.

The following day dawned clear and cold. Connal Lee's adopted cousins took extra care in their grooming, honored to be invited to such an important council of war. White Wolf and Short Rainbow wrapped Screaming Eagle's long braids with mink fur held in place with beaded ribbons of dyed doeskin. They carefully inserted ceremonial notched eagle feathers in his hair, each notch denoting a tribal enemy killed in battle. Screaming Eagle proudly lifted his war bonnet onto his head when they finished.

White Wolf surprised Connal Lee when he combed his long braids free. His shiny, lush black hair spread over his back and shoulders, slightly curly from being braided. Short Rainbow wound a thin ribbon of doeskin, died bright blue and beaded with faceted blue glass trade beads around a single strand of his hair. The lock hung down beside his right eye. She inserted an eagle feather dyed blue at the top of the tuft of hair. She had cut it flat, so it stuck up like a brush. Connal Lee hardly recognized his handsome adopted cousin. White Wolf's clothing had been beaded with blue dyed porcupine quills in elegant symbolic patterns.

Short Rainbow decked herself out in her finest clothing of bleached white doeskin. She had trimmed her soft smock's shoulders, arms, chest, and back with beaded bands of two-inch white porcupine quills in rows of geometric patterns. She wore a doeskin headband around her forehead, lined with vertical white quills like a crown. Her leggings and moccasins continued the solid white beading. After she finished dressing, she lifted a necklace of bright red mountain laurel seeds out of a small leather envelope and draped them around her neck. She had traded for the bright red seeds from far away to the south and strung them on a buffalo sinew to make the necklace. Connal Lee thought she looked so glorious that he had to give her a hug.

"You beautiful, so beautiful." Short Rainbow beamed at his compliment.

They saddled their horses and rode to Chief SoYo'Cant's tipi in the center of the encampment. The Chief came out to join them. White Dove had groomed his hair for the formal meeting by dividing it into three parts. She had braided the two sides halfway up. Above the braids, his lush, thick hair hung loose in soft pillows. She had pulled the top center segment into a ponytail that hung down his back. She had greased the front to stand in a proud pompadour before weaving it into a four-way flat braid. She had decorated the braid with dyed porcupine quill beads strung on Indian hemp strings. The Chief wore his proud breastplate over finely beaded clothing. He also wore silver and turquoise rings on all eight fingers, traded over the years with Navajo craftsmen from far away to the south in Mexican territory.

Connal Lee enjoyed seeing how his native family enjoyed dressing up so elaborately for ceremonial occasions. He hadn't witnessed their vanity before. He felt quite drab by comparison.

White Dove followed the Chief out of his tent, ceremoniously carrying his long war bonnet. After the Chief mounted his great white war stallion, she handed him the war bonnet with a smile and a bow. Soon Arimo, Teniwaaten, and the counselors rode up, also wearing their finest. Screaming Eagle led the small parade through the Fort's gate and east to Beehive House. They arrived to find more than a dozen horses and five buggies tied up to the chain hitching posts lining the avenue. They found space for their horses in front of Lion House. Chief SoYo'Cant, War Chief Red Fighter, and Screaming Eagle proudly lifted off their great war bonnets and secured them behind their saddles. Bright red and yellow leaves topped the young trees lining the street. When they reached the Governor's mansion, the gate in the rock wall stood open. They entered and found Brigham Young and several men in military uniforms and business suits waiting for them on the broad porch that extended the entire width of the mansion.

Brigham Young smiled as he passed among them, shaking their hands and greeting them by name. He welcomed the elderly counselors Chief SoYo'Cant had brought with him. "Chief Arimo, gentlemen, please accompany me a short distance to the Endowment House

74

on Temple Square. It has a meeting room large enough for us to be comfortable."

The delegation followed Brigham Young past the corral for the horses of the Nauvoo Legion and the tithing office to the meeting place. As they crossed Temple Square, Connal Lee noticed tiny green sprouts poking above the ground. He looked more closely and recognized winter wheat. Brigham Young unlocked the door to a small wing south of the neat two-story adobe brick building. He showed them through to a good-sized whitewashed meeting room. The room held a lectern raised up two steps on a stage so everyone in the audience could see the speaker. It stood in front of rows of simple, varnished pine pews.

Brigham Young strode up to the podium and watched as everyone found seats. Teniwaaten sat between Chief SoYo'Cant and his War Chief. The Chief's two elderly counselors sat directly behind the Chief so they could lean forward, one on each side of Teniwaaten's head, and listen in as he translated the proceedings. Connal Lee sat beside Short Rainbow. White Wolf sat between Screaming Eagle and Arimo to translate for them.

"Gentlemen. Please take your seats where you wish. We are all here to share information, so we will not stand on ceremony. Since this podium has the best acoustics to reach the audience, please step up and make your reports from here so everyone can hear." He waited until everyone settled in and gave him their attention. "As Governor of the Territory of Utah, I officially call this council of war to order. We welcome our valued allies, Chief Arimo of the Shoshone Nation and his counselors, as our honored guests. I also want to extend a welcome to the officers of the territorial militia and the good citizens of Great Salt Lake City who have joined us here this morning. Let us begin by inviting the Honorable Abraham Smoot, the second mayor of Great Salt Lake City, to the podium to tell us how he discovered the nefarious attack by President Buchanan and how he brought word back to us here in Zion."

Connal Lee watched a tall, slender, nicely dressed man stand up in the audience. He placed his hat and gloves on his bench seat and strode up to the front of the room. The Mayor's hair had turned nearly white. He wore a neatly trimmed white beard with the mustache completely shaved off. His bushy white eyebrows pulled up in a frown as he focused on delivering his report. The Mayor shook hands with Brigham Young, then stepped up to the podium. He coughed into his fist and looked up. "Governor Young, Chief Arimo, distinguished guests, and fellow citizens of Great Salt Lake City, thank you for this opportunity to report on our last trip to Independence, Missouri. You might know that last year, the church formed the Brigham Young Express and Carrying Company. It quickly became known as the Y. X. Company, short for the Young Express Company. The business bid for and received a four-year contract for monthly mail service between Independence and Great Salt Lake City."

Mayor Smoot coughed into his fist, again, to clear his throat, then grabbed the lectern with both hands. "As both mayor and an officer of the Y. X. Company, I led my companions, Orrin Porter Rockwell and Judson Stoddard, on a routine mail run east along the Mormon Trail. We departed the first day of July. While traveling east, we became curious when we passed huge wagon trains heading west on the Overland Trail. Two trains of sixty-two wagons each, to be precise. When we arrived in Independence, we learned that the federal government had canceled the mail contract to our great dismay. The postmaster went on to tell us that President Buchanan had ordered twenty-five hundred federal troops to the Utah Territories. The government had also contracted with a large company of professional teamsters to transport vast quantities of supplies to support the ground troops. We couldn't find out anything more about the army's orders, so we replenished our supplies and departed west as quickly as we could manage. Once out of sight of civilization, we drove the livestock relentlessly. We stopped at the supply stations only long enough to harness fresh mule teams. We slept in the wagon as we pressed on, night and day, taking turns in the driver's seat.

"We arrived late the evening of the twenty-third of July. The next day we found the governor celebrating the tenth anniversary of arriving in this great valley, up in Big Cottonwood Canyon, with a crowd of around twenty-six hundred Saints. We immediately pulled the governor aside and gave him our report. Governor Young didn't want to dampen the merry event, so he waited until nightfall to announce what we knew of the government's designs." Mayor Smoot paused a moment, then looked back at Brigham Young sitting on a chair behind him. "I believe that sums it up, Governor. I return the pulpit to you, sir."

"Thank you, Mister Mayor. Well, Chief Arimo and valued allies, for whatever reason, President Buchanan has still not sent word of his plans to me, the Territorial Governor, as would have been the proper procedure in the case of any complaints or accusations against us. The government never held hearings to determine the facts here on the frontier, as would have been proper procedure. However, we've since learned from our own reconnaissance missions that Buchanan sent a new territorial governor, new federal judges, and armed troops to enforce federal law in our beloved territory. On August the fifteenth, I declared martial law in the entire territory. At that time, nearly all the gentile business owners left the city to go on to California or return to the States.

"In the communique that accompanied the proclamation of martial law, I ordered all officers and commanders of the Nauvoo Legion, let there be no excitement. Save life always when possible. We do not wish to shed a drop of blood if it can be avoided. This course will give us great influence abroad.

"On that same day of August the fifteenth, I ordered Colonel Robert Burton to take a unit of one-hundred twenty-five men along the eastern routes to the valley. I commanded them to observe the American regiments marching towards the territory and protect any Mormon immigrants still traveling the Overland Trail.

"When the Colonel's spy mission encountered the troops, he sent two of his men into the soldier's camps pretending they were travelers from California on their way back to the States. They mingled with the boastful uniformed soldiers for a day and a night. They came away understanding the army had orders to hang the leaders of the Mormon Church and to free our women from being forced into unlawful marriages. With the way the men bragged about how they would liberate our wives, it became clear they planned nothing more than looting, rape, and general mayhem. We know, now, that those common foot soldiers did not have the right of it, but the Colonel became alarmed at this new intelligence."

Brigham Young paused and poured water into a glass on the podium. He sipped the water as he listened to the murmur of translators catch up. "After twenty-seven years of persecution back east, we assumed the worst. We have been driven from our homes twice in Missouri and once in Illinois at the point of the bayonet and with the aid of state authorities. Only thirteen years ago, we buried our beloved prophet, Joseph Smith, after a mob killed him in the Carthage Jail while supposedly under the protection of the governor of Illinois. Only two months before then, in May of this year, Parley P. Pratt, one of our Twelve Apostles, was murdered in Arkansas. We dispatched diplomatic envoys to Washington with instructions to find and negotiate a peaceful solution. But, we did not leave things to the vagaries of diplomatic channels.

"We immediately sent word recalling our settlers from distant homesteads such as San Bernardino and Carson Valley to the west. We sent word ordering all missionaries to return from the Eastern States and Europe. We gathered guns and ammunition and stepped up the manufacture of Colt revolvers. We cached our grain and other food supplies against the possibility of a mass exodus. We dispatched units of armed guards north, south, and west to secure all access routes into the territory. We are currently building fortifications in Echo Canyon and East Canyon to block the American Army from entering the valley if and when they make it that far. We formulated contingency plans for burning all the crops and homes and evacuating north about five-hundred miles to Fort Owen in Bitterroot Valley, up in the Territory of Oregon. Fort Owen lies about three hundred miles north of Fort Hall, further north than Fort Lemhi. I ordered the sale and trading of foodstuffs to be restricted to Church members only. We could no longer afford to supply provisions to wagon trains passing through on their way to California or Oregon.

"Now, Colonel Burton, sir. Would you kindly step forward and share the defensive tactics we have planned to date with our allies?"

Colonel Burton stood up, placed his hat on his seat, and marched up to the podium in a crisp, military manner. He shook hands with Brigham Young and took the pulpit. The Governor sat down in one of several chairs lining the wall behind the podium. "Thank you, Governor. Chief Arimo, fellow allies, gentlemen of the Nauvoo Legion, and good citizens of Great Salt Lake City. His Excellency the Governor, the commander of our territorial militia, ordered us to put on our thinking caps and come up with ways to delay the army's advance without spilling a single drop of blood. As the Governor declared, not shedding any blood will impress the politicians and newspapermen back east. So, we developed a multi-pronged defense.

"We took a page from the guerilla warfare tactics developed fifty years ago when the Spanish came up against the superior forces of Napoleon during the Peninsular War. Our situation today is not dissimilar. We combined those techniques with the scorched earth policy used so successfully against Napoleon when he invaded Tsarist Russia. Scorched earth policy is when one destroys any assets that could aid and abet the enemy, like food, water, animal fodder, and buildings.

"We assembled an irregular cavalry of mounted men without uniforms of any kind. We refer to them as scouts, scoundrels, and bandits – never officers or soldiers. They traveled east under the command of Captain Lot Smith. Their orders were to ride eastward towards High Pass and intercept the foot soldiers and their supply trains as far away east of here as they could manage. They were ordered to do everything possible to annoy and harass the army in every way they could. Stampeding their livestock at night. Burning the grassy plains so they couldn't feed their livestock. Staging nightly ambushes so the soldiers couldn't sleep at night. Burning their supply wagons. Blocking their trail with fallen trees. Destroying all the fords and bridges so they couldn't cross rivers and streams. Delay. Delay. Delay. They remain out there today, making hit and run attacks but always retreating before the army can muster their men and fire in defense.

"Why, on October the fifth, alone, Captain Smith led his men on three raids in different places. They found the army and their supply wagons and cannons spread out, not traveling as one large group but rather in small clusters. The supply wagons did not have any cavalry or army protection. Our fine irregulars burned seventy-six wagons and ran off a great many of the army's draft mules. One of the groups he attacked was carrying winter coats for the commissary. Captain Smith received badly needed warm coats for his men. This winter is colder than usual, which hinders the army's progress, but makes it hard on our men, too. He invited the teamsters to take only what they could carry, then ordered the wagons burned. He sent a couple of his men to herd all the oxen back to us here in the Great Basin.

"Our men were ordered never to fire their weapons at the invaders. They could harass and hinder the army but never engage in a battle nor take any life. Already the high passes are freezing, making the foot soldiers' lives more miserable. Nature is helping us delay them even further.

"With the grass burned for a mile on each side of the trail, the army supply trains can't find forage for all their livestock. The teamsters are nearly ready to revolt and break their contracts rather than lose their wagons and draft animals, their livelihood. Our irregular cavalry of scoundrels has been serenading the soldiers at night using tin pans and baking oven lids for musical instruments. The noise effectively keeps the men awake and stampedes their pack mules and officers' horses. We sent circulars into the frozen, hungry camps, offering fifty dollars and safe passage to California for any who did not wish to fight and die for their country in an unjust war. About four hundred men accepted the offer and deserted."

The Colonel paused while the men before him chuckled and slapped each other on the back. When the translators fell silent, he concluded. "The now Brevet Brigadier General Johnston replaced Colonel Edmund Alexander as commander back on the fifth of October. He immediately ordered his men to depart for Fort Bridger. Fort Bridger lies only a hundred and twenty-some miles east of Great Salt Lake City. Now, back in fifty-three, some of the Mormons who settled the area accused Jim Bridger of selling liquor and weapons to the Indians in violation of federal law. Governor Young, the Indian Agent for the Territory of Utah, sent the Nauvoo Legion. They took over the Fort, then built Fort Supply about twelve miles south to service our Mormon immigrants. When the governor heard of the army's plans to establish the general's headquarters at Fort Bridger for the invasion of Utah, he sent the Mormon Militia under Wild Bill Hickman and his brother to burn both Forts.

"Johnston reached the main body of the army camped on Ham's Fork of the Green River early in November. He had Jim Bridger guiding him as an army employee with the pay grade of a major. The General brought more troops and supplies with him. He ordered the entire army to advance towards Fort Bridger, committed to entering Great Salt Lake City according to his written orders. The popular officer worked at motivating his discouraged men to overcome their many reverses caused by Indians and what he referred to as those damned Mormon mountaineers.

"The general broke camp on November the sixth and led his men forward across the open barren desert where they found no shelter from the winter winds and storms. They only had stunted sagebrush for fuel. The army and their trains stretched out for fifteen miles. Once well underway, a severe winter storm overcame them. Snow and sleet blew in their faces. They couldn't see. They goaded their teams until they dropped dead in their harnesses and yokes. It took them fifteen miserable days to travel a mere thirty-five miles. Soldiers had to pull the wagons themselves at the end, making up for the loss of livestock to the Indians, the weather, and our irregular cavalry. Then, they arrived to find the two burned-out forts.

"Johnston reluctantly ordered his army to winter there. He could see that it would be impossible to reach our lovely valley before spring. He set his men to work building a temporary camp of tents and improvised shelters two miles south of the ruins of Fort Bridger. They named it Fort Scott. In addition to his army personnel, they had another twenty-five hundred teamsters, blacksmiths, suppliers, and other civilian auxiliaries and hangers-on. Their expansive tent city currently holds five thousand men poised to descend into the valley here.

"Johnston sent his men to the abandoned Mormon farms in Green River Valley, twelve miles southwest of Fort Bridger at Fort Supply. The Mormons had harvested their crops and cached their food underground before abandoning Fort Supply. Governor Cumming, his wife, the freighters, camp followers, and the army are currently enjoying a miserable winter with no shelter and very little food.

"So far, Captain Smith and his irregulars have torched seventy-four wagons carrying three months' worth of supplies for the isolated army. They have captured fourteen-hundred of the two-thousand head of cattle sent to supply the army with milk and meat during the winter.

"We intend to continue these delaying tactics all through this winter and coming spring, making the invading soldier's lives as miserable as possible and delaying them at every turn. Now, does anyone have any questions?"

Colonel Burton paused and looked at Chief Arimo and his delegation. Connal Lee raised his hand like in class. "Yes, young man with the Shoshone Delegation."

Connal Lee stood up self-consciously as all eyes turned on him. "Yes, suh..." He didn't get any further before he heard a couple of men call out, "Louder. We can't hear you." Connal Lee coughed in his fist, embarrassed. Imitating Captain Hanover's loud public speaking voice, he began again. "Yes, suh. Thanks. My name is Connal Lee Swinton. Ah am the adopted son of Chief Arimo, Chief of all the Shoshone nation. During this meeting, Ah got to thinking. From what Ah've been told, a country's armed forces exist to protect the citizens from aggressions by enemies. Is this typical for the United States armed forces to be sent to attack American citizens in a Territory of the United States? Aren't the Mormons here in the Territory of Utah American citizens? Doesn't the American flag fly over every city in the Territory?"

Colonel Burton frowned. "Well, young man, you raise a most perplexing question. I'm a graduate of West Point, Class of twenty-nine. I studied the history of warfare in the Americas. To the best of my knowledge, this is the first time armed forces have been sent against our country's own citizens. In other countries, when this happens, we call it a civil war. Civil wars occur when one group of people wishes to throw off the rule of the powers in charge. Since we are not in rebellion, this action can't be called a civil war, but it is definitely the first time we have ever seen such a thing happen. We in the Nauvoo Legion sincerely hope this will not set a precedent for attacking fellow American citizens. Thank you for your thoughtful question, Mister Swinton."

Colonel Burton looked at the other Shoshone delegates and the rest of the audience. "Any further questions, gentlemen? No? Very well then. Thank you for your attention, gentlemen. Governor Young, I turn the podium back over to you, sir."

Brigham Young thanked the Colonel, then opened up the floor to comments, ideas, and recommendations. They spent another three hours reviewing the details of their plans in depth before Brigham Young thanked everyone for attending and contributing to their deliberations. He then closed the council of war.

Chief SoYo'Cant walked towards Brigham Young with Teniwaaten close at his shoulder to translate. The Chief congratulated Brigham Young on a brilliant if unconventional strategy of pursuing the imminent war. "Whenever we Shoshone can help in the upcoming war, please send messengers to find me. I will winter in my clan's base camp on the shores of the Portneuf River just south of Fort Hall. We will do whatever we can to advance your bloodless war and maintain peace across our sacred hunting grounds. Your idea of a war without any fighting is foreign to my experience and way of thinking, but perhaps you have the right of it. Your plan just might work out as you hope. Good luck, Chief Brigham Young."

"Thank you, Chief Arimo. Likewise, sir, if we can be of service to you and your fine people, please do not hesitate to let me know. You have been a good ally, almost our only ally, in fact, for these past ten years. For that, you have my sincere thanks and admiration. Good luck to you and all your people, Chief Arimo."

Screaming Eagle led the Shoshone delegation to their horses in front of Beehive House. They rushed back to their camp for a late midday meal.

Connal Lee's mind swirled with the military strategies he had heard about, so different from how he understood armies met head-on in glorious battle as told in stories. Attending Brigham Young's council of war reaffirmed his deep desire to grow up to be a strong warrior for the Shoshone and perhaps even an officer in the cavalry, too, like his hero, Captain Reed. He also discovered he liked being in the center of things, in the know, part of the action.

That evening Connal Lee ate supper in Chief SoYo'Cant's tipi. Teniwaaten sat beside him so they could discuss the council of war they had attended earlier in the day.

Teniwaaten took almost all of his meals with the Chief's family. White Wolf had explained to Connal Lee when they first arrived in the camp that Teniwaaten had no wives, husbands, or children to help him in his life. He had never invited a woman, man, or two-spirit member of the tribe to his bed as a lover or spouse. White Wolf described how years before the arrival of the Long Knives, Chief SoYo'Cant arranged for his intelligent and curious young nephew to serve the Black Robes, the Jesuits, at their Cataldo Mission.

"The chief had heard how white men encroached and settled by the water sources, not moving on like the Newe and our fellow tribes have for centuries. When the chief's clan traded with tribes to the north and east of our traditional hunting grounds, he heard all the stories. It caused him great concern. He worried about the problem and met with his counselors about it. Finally, he led our entire tribe on a fifty-five-day journey far to the north of here to visit the Cataldo Mission, taking his nephew to learn from the Black Robes.

"In return for the boy's services, the priests promised to teach Teniwaaten English and French, history, mathematics, and the ways of the Europeans. They required a peace treaty with the Iroquois and Coeur d'Alene tribes, whom the Jesuits served, in repayment for the boy's education. From that day until this, the Shoshone and Iroquois share safe conduct through each nations' lands.

"Five years passed before the youth returned to Chief SoYo'Cant. His teachers had mistreated him. They had beaten him regularly for the slightest mistake in his chores or studies. They had given him hard duties and fed him poorly. Yet, the young boy managed to learn, despite the ill-treatment.

"Even though the boy politely informed the priests he was not a berdache, they forced sex on him and abused him in the dark of night. When he fought back or complained, the Black Robes boxed his ears and ordered him to stay in his place and do what he was told. After they finished using the boy, they ordered him to go to confession the next morning to be forgiven of his sins and shortcomings so that all would be made right. Their mistreatment of him before he experienced his own sexual awakening apparently broke something in his soul. He has never been able to find enjoyment in the act of making love with a man, a woman, or a berdache to this day.

"Fortunately, the Jesuits could not stamp out their young ward's great curiosity and brilliant mind. He grew up conversant in English and French. He also learned all the right manners and customs to confidently move in European and American society. Chief SoYo'Cant welcomed him back to the clan and invited him to tutor the tribe's children. The chief wished his people to learn how to communicate directly with the Long Knives without needing interpreters. After that day, they called the young man Teniwaaten, which means teacher."

After they finished eating, Connal Lee looked over at Teniwaaten. "What are diplomatic envoys, Teniwaaten?"

"Hm. That is not an easy one to answer, Connal Lee. You see, among the nations of the world, there often arise conflicts. When kings, dictators, or presidents have standing armies, they often want to enforce their imperious wishes by force of arms. Men die when that happens. Diplomats are people from one country who know the language and customs of another country and, more importantly, can gain access to that country's rulers and decision-makers. Kings send these delegates and envoys to negotiate a settlement of the conflicts or demands without resorting to force of arms.

"To bring the idea down to a more personal level and apply it to our immediate situation, Connal Lee, we have three primary sources of power in these frontier territories today. The Mormons wield the greatest influence in the region because they outnumber everyone else. The Mormon Church's leaders are the most powerful men among their growing group.

"Then we have our local Plains Indian tribes. The largest tribe today is our northern Shoshone tribe. Chief SoYo'Cant is the most powerful man in our tribe. He is a leader whom other clans and tribes turn to for advice. He is a strong, wise leader.

"The third power center in the area is the armed forces of the United States of America. Right now, the army is split into two commands. We have the cavalry charged with protecting travelers on the Overland Trail and keeping the local Indian tribes under control. They are mobile and well-armed, but they are small in number compared to Mormons and our Indian tribes. Second, we have General Johnston and his army of two-thousand five-hundred American foot soldiers, all armed with rifles, handguns, and enormous cannons. Because of their vastly superior number of weapons, they are a force that can threaten both the Mormons and the tribes."

"Do you see where I'm going with this, Connal Lee?"

Connal Lee nodded, his forehead creased in concentration. "Ah think maybe Ah'm beginning to."

"I see in you, someone qualified to negotiate with all three power centers converging on our sacred hunting grounds. You are intelligent. You are mobile and know how to take care of yourself while traveling. You are well-armed. You have been adopted as our Chief's son, so you can gain access to the chiefs and councils of other tribes and clans. You have the ear of your adopted father. You are friends with Captain Reed and Lieutenant Anderson based in Fort Laramie. They have the ear of the major in command of the safety of the Overland Trail from Missouri to trails' end in the Territories of Oregon, Utah, or California.

"Chief SoYo'Cant introduced you to Brigham Young, the most powerful Mormon, as his adopted son. If you needed to reach Brigham Young to deliver requests for aid or to make offers of assistance, they would admit you into his presence as the chief's adopted son and envoy. You speak his language, so he could listen to your message and understand you clearly."

Teniwaaten reached out and rested a hand on Connal Lee's shoulder. When Connal Lee looked up and made eye contact, Teniwaaten nodded approvingly. "You are uniquely positioned to be of great service to all three centers of power converging on our land. We all see war looming on the horizon. You can gain access to and communicate clearly with all the decision-makers when the need arises. I believe you will play an important role in saving the lives of Indians, Mormons, and soldiers."

"Wow, that's a big responsibility, Teniwaaten. What do Ah need to do so I can help keep the peace?"

"Chief SoYo'Cant and I discussed this opportunity on the way back from the council of war. Continue what you have already begun, Connal Lee. Perfect your communication skills. Expand your vocabulary in Shoshone and in English. Cultivate your relationships with the leaders and decision-makers who will lead us to war or peace in the near future. Earn and keep their trust by being truthful and honorable in all your dealings with every man. Everything else will come naturally as events unfold."

"Y'all sure have given me a lot to think about this evening. Thanks for explaining it all to me. Well, Ah think it's time Ah rejoined my family. Good night and thanks again." Connal Lee leaned down and gave Teniwaaten a gentle hug before he said good night to Chief SoYo'Cant.

A very thoughtful young boy walked north through the camp that evening until he reached Short Rainbow's welcome tipi.

The following day, Screaming Eagle led his family to accompany Connal Lee to Provo. They arrived before the sun had completely set. Connal Lee inquired at Fort Utah on the west side of the little town of Provo and received directions to Captain Hanover's homes down on the river. The Captain's first and third wives had supper ready when Connal Lee knocked on their door. A pretty young girl opened the door. Connal Lee introduced himself. "May Ah please see Captain Hanover?"

The girl glared suspiciously at his Shoshone friends but invited them in any way. "Come on in. I'll call Papa. Please wait in here."

Captain Hanover's eyes lit up when he saw Connal Lee standing in his parlor holding a big leather hat in his hands. The Captain rushed over and enthusiastically shook his hand. "Connal Lee! Baby Boy! Yer alive. I'm so happy t' see ya again, young man. We were worried plumb t' death about ya. But jus' look at ya now, standin' there bold as brass an' lookin' all growed up, t' boot. Now, who're these friends ya brought with ya?"

Connal Lee made introductions. The Captain's young third wife heard them talking and walked in to find out who had come calling. Connal Lee recognized her when she entered the room. He walked over and shook her hand. "How are y'all doing, Sister Hanover? It's nice to see y'all again."

"Well, I'm certainly glad t' see you, too. We were so worried about you when you didn't return after the Crow war party attacked us." She turned to her husband. "Dear, we have supper ready. I can set four more places if you would like t' invite your guests t' join us."

"Excellent idea, me darlin'. Won't ya please come join us fer supper, Connal Lee? This'll give us time fer ya t' tell us all about yer big adventures."

Connal Lee looked at his adopted cousins. White Wolf nodded his head affirmative. Connal Lee smiled at the captain. "We would be pleased to join y'all for supper, Captain Hanover. Thanks for the invitation."

The Captain's young wife rushed into the dining room and added more plates to their long trestle dining table. The Captain pointed to his big Victorian hall tree next to the entrance door. "Please hang up yer hats an' weapons an' come join us. Welcome t' Fort Utah, everybody."

During supper, Connal Lee told of getting wounded. He praised the Shoshone family for healing him and protecting him. Later, he asked if the Captain knew the whereabouts of Zeff and Sister Woman. His face fell when he heard they had stayed on at Fort Hall to homestead a clay claim. "Dang it all! Now, Ah'll have to travel all the way back to Fort Hall before Ah can see them. It feels like we will never be reunited."

"No worry, Connal Lee. We happy travel with you to Fort Hall while Chief SoYo'Cant trade furs."

"Thanks so much, White Wolf. Y'all have been so good to me. Well, Captain, what can y'all tell me about Sister Baines and Brother Baines? Did they come here to Fort Utah with y'all?"

"Nope. Sorry, Connal Lee. They liked the looks o' the young orchards along the foothills back north o' Great Salt Lake City. They decided t' try the little farmin' settlement o' Bountiful fer a time. I'm sure ya will find 'em there. Bountiful's about five miles north o' Great Salt Lake City, doncha know. It used t' be called Sessions Settlement. Then they changed it to the North Canyon Ward. They renamed the little town a couple o' years ago after a place mentioned in the Book o' Mormon as a lush land flowing with fruit an' honey. If ya leave early tomorrow, ya can be there by suppertime tomorrow evenin', easy. Now, please be our guests an' spend the night in our home."

Connal Lee looked at White Wolf, who answered for them. "Thank you, Captain. We not use to white man bed. We sleep outside under stars like always. Thank you."

They talked late into the night. Connal Lee told the captain he had grown fond of the dark brown mare the captain had loaned him for hunting. "Could Ah buy her from y'all, please? Ah would like to keep her."

The Captain sat back in his chair. "Well, sir. In point o' fact, she belongs t' the Church's Perpetual Emigration Fund. However, I would be more than happy t' accept yer payment on the Fund's behalf. Now, what can ya afford t' pay, Connal Lee?"

"Well, what do you think she's worth?"

"I seem t' recall payin' a hundred bucks when I bought 'er."

"That sounds fair. And the packhorse?"

"Oh, sixty bucks should do."

Connal Lee reached into a leather pouch fastened to his knife belt and pulled out a fistful of ten-dollar gold coins. Each thin one-inch diameter disc contained half an ounce of gold. He counted out sixteen bright, shiny Liberty Head coins and pushed them across the table towards the Captain. The Captain looked up, astonished that Connal Lee carried that much money on him. "Now, where on earth did ya come up with that much cash money, Connal Lee?"

"Oh, Ah had a bit of good fortune when we fought some Crow invaders back up northeast of here. Their furs brought a pretty penny at the Fort Hall trading post."

"A pretty penny, indeed. Well, thanks fer settlin' up accounts. The mare an' packhorse are yers. Before ya leave, I'll write ya up a bill o' sale."

"Great. Thanks, Captain Hanover. Now, what about that shotgun y'all lent me back on the trail?"

The Captain gazed at Connal Lee, then nodded his head. "Ya did us a big service, selflessly goin' out after a long day's journey an' huntin' fresh meat night after night. The way I figure it, ya earned that shotgun fair an' square with all yer hard work. Keep it with the thanks of all the company an' the Emigration Fund, Connal Lee."

"Why, thanks very much, Captain. Much obliged."

When Captain Hanover yawned, Connal Lee stood up and said good night. He led his friends outside to their furs for the night.

Shortly after sunrise, Connal Lee and his adopted Shoshone cousins joined Captain Hanover and his family for a hearty breakfast of bacon and fried eggs. The family passed around slices of freshly baked hot bread and clay jars of apple butter. When they finished eating, they thanked the captain and his first and third wives for their hospitality and said their goodbyes.

They stopped at Chief SoYo'Cant's tipi long enough to advise him they would travel on to Bountiful, then head back north to Fort Hall to find Connal Lee's brother and sister. The Chief complained that nearly all the trading posts and manufacturing shops were closed due to the war. The non-Mormon shopkeepers had returned to the States or moved on to California. The Mormon merchants had taken their goods and moved south below Provo. "I'm afraid this trip is a waste, at least as far as finding provisions for my people. Well, good-bye, son. We will return back to our winter quarters shortly, as well."

Connal Lee and his family loaded up their packhorses and put lead reins on Connal Lee's victory horses. It took an hour, but Short Rainbow and her sisters loaded up her beautifully decorated tipi on four big travoises. They loaded up the family's stores on three more travoises. Finally, they had everything organized and took off riding northerly at a walking pace.

They rode through the south gate, still missing its doors, into the unfinished adobe fort surrounding the small community of Bountiful. They stopped at the general store on Main Street just south of Center Street and asked after the Baines. Clouds glowed pink and gold from the sun as it slid down behind a lovely mountain named Antelope Island just offshore in the vast lake. The storekeeper gave them directions to a log cabin the Baines had rented until they found a plot to homestead.

The four of them rode further up into the foothills, following Mill Creek until they came upon a simple log cabin. Connal Lee recognized the Baines' handcart resting in front of the one-room cottage by Lorna's hand-painted lettering, *Carpe Diem*. Smoke rose from a stone chimney opposite the door. Suddenly in a hurry, Connal Lee hopped down off his pretty brown mare and knocked briskly on the door. He took off his hat and riding gloves and held them in his left hand. The door opened. Lorna Baines' hand flew up to her mouth. She shouted, "Connal Lee! Look, dear! It's Connal Lee returned from the grave. Come in, Baby Boy. Come in!"

Connal Lee rushed up and gave her a big hug. Gilbert walked out in his stocking feet. "Oh! Connal Lee! We've been so worried." He swept Connal Lee and Lorna into a great bear hug. Connal Lee couldn't help it. He burst out crying from joy and from relief in finding his foster parents alive and well. When his tears turned to laughter, he pulled away from the three-way hug. Finally, he remembered his manners. He gestured towards his Shoshone cousins, dismounting their large warhorses, and introduced everyone. He couldn't stop smiling.

Lorna welcomed them to her home. "I would invite you in, but there's no room inside. We'll come sit outside with you. We're used to sitting on the ground while chatting with Connal Lee. It's what we did for months on the trail before he disappeared. Isn't that right, son?"

Connal Lee helped his Shoshone family unsaddle their riding horses and unload the packhorses. They worked as a team to unhitch the great travois and lower them to the ground for the night.

Gilbert pulled on his worn hiking boots and helped his Shoshone guests build a fire. He had a store of well-cured firewood stacked beside the cabin for fuel. Lorna invited them all to sit down and relax while she cooked supper. She rushed into her tiny home and brought out a Dutch oven and frying pan. After they ate supper, the happy group spent the evening catching up until sleep overcame them. The Baines retired to their simple bed in the cabin while Connal Lee joined his cousins in their sleeping furs.

Over coffee and fresh pan-fried cornbread for breakfast, Connal Lee announced they would leave soon for Fort Hall to find Zeff and Sister Woman. Lorna and Gilbert shared a look, then they both nodded at each other. Lorna focused on Connal Lee. "We've been talking about how lovely we found the Snake River basin outside Fort Hall. As nice as Bountiful is, it's still just desert here. They never finished and secured the fortifications. Yes, Bountiful has canyons and rivers coming down out of the mountains. The farmers have diverted the river water with irrigation ditches to water the orchards and gardens on the foothills and the fields lower down in the valley. But we don't find anything nearly as welcoming here as the Snake River lowlands outside Fort Hall. If we wouldn't hold you back too much, we would love to accompany you back to Brother and Sister Swinton's clay claim."

Connal Lee looked both surprised and pleased. He offered to lend them horses to ride so they wouldn't have to push their handcart. "You do know how to ride, don't you, Mother Baines?"

"Of course I do, silly. That surely does sound nicer than walking, doesn't it, dear?"

Gilbert nodded his head with a big smile on his face.

It only took a couple of hours to prepare. White Wolf and Short Rainbow jury-rigged a harness so one of the packhorses could pull the Baines' handcart. They helped pack up Lorna and Gilbert's belongings, then loaded their own packhorses. Connal Lee offered the Baines two of his stallions with ornately beaded Crow saddles. They took off traveling cross country around ten that morning. The packhorse pulling the handcart reacted skittishly at having something following behind him, rumbling and bouncing along. But it soon became used to the noise and settled down.

"This is just like old times, isn't it, Mother Baines? Ah'm so glad we found y'all at last. Ah've missed y'all so much over the past months. So much. Y'all will never know."

Chapter 9: First Love

Their small caravan took the trip at a slow horses' walk, slowed down even further by the seven great travoises carrying Short Rainbow's tipi, their luggage, tools, supplies, and all their stores of foods laid up for winter. When they stopped for their noon break, Lorna and Gilbert both struggled to dismount. Lorna chuckled, a little embarrassed. "Well. It *has* been a long time since I rode. I guess I'm not so young and nimble anymore, either. And it's not because I'm riding straddle after almost always riding sidesaddle. I'm just simply out of practice riding!"

Gilbert stepped over and pulled her into a hug. "I'm not in shape for riding, either, me love. It *has* been a couple of years or more since we last went riding, hasn't it, just?"

Connal Lee glanced at his foster parents, then at White Wolf. "We're not in any rush, are we, White Wolf? Why don't we take a long rest before moving on?"

Short Rainbow distributed slices of venison jerky with a bit of pemmican on the side for their cold travel meal. Lorna looked at the small portion of prepared meat curiously. "What is this, Connal Lee?"

"Oh. That's what the Indians call pemmican, Mother Baines. It's dried meat mixed with fat and dried nuts, fruits, and berries. Sometimes they sweeten it with wild honey or sap from maple trees. It's right tasty."

She took a bite. She didn't care for it, but she found it sweet and chewy, so she ate it. She didn't want to offend Short Rainbow.

They resumed their slow journey. When they arrived outside the walled fort of the small township of Farmington, a mere seven miles north of Bountiful, they set up camp for the night. Connal Lee looked west at Antelope Island rising out of the Great Salt Lake. He turned and gazed east at the looming Wasatch Mountain Range and decided to try his luck hunting up in the foothills. Leading his packhorse behind him, he took off riding easterly. The rest of his party set up camp. The Baines pitched their small tent just as they had on the Overland Trail. Connal Lee returned an hour and a half later with a young doe for their supper.

Connal Lee helped Short Rainbow skin and butcher the doe. Lorna helped Short Rainbow fry up enough steaks for their party of six. Lorna shared some cornbread leftover from breakfast. The Shoshone weren't used to cornbread but ate it anyway. White Wolf found it dry and stale but shrugged and finished his serving.

That night, Connal Lee snuggled up to his Shoshone cousins. He leaned across Screaming Eagle's strong body and hugged Short Rainbow. Short Rainbow returned his embrace. Connal Lee gently entered her, enjoying the naturally slippery hold on his strong erection. He began thrusting and withdrawing. He felt strong hands massaging his back and buttocks, encouraging him on. Screaming Eagle slid his big warm hand between Connal Lee and Short Rainbow and played with their nipples, pushing them to higher and higher sensual delights.

Lorna and Gilbert, trying to sleep in their quilts on the other side of the dwindling fire, couldn't help but notice all the rhythmically writhing bodies under the sleeping furs. They looked at each other in the dim light. Gilbert winked, then hugged Lorna closer. He whispered in her ear, "Ah, to be young, again."

Lorna just sighed.

Half an hour later, Connal Lee and Short Rainbow clasped each other tightly as they concluded their blissful union within moments of each other, sighing happily, breathing each other's breath. They fell apart after Connal Lee's erection went down and withdrew from her, naturally. Connal Lee ended up being hugged by Screaming Eagle. Short Rainbow found herself pulled into a loving embrace by White Wolf. After a few minutes, Short Rainbow muttered affectionately, "Thank you, Connal Lee. I believe you might have just been the one who planted the seed of a boy child in my womb. I do believe I am seeing a true vision of a child resulting from our beautiful lovemaking this night. I see a strong son of pale skin with black hair. Not as pale as your skin, Connal Lee, but paler than ours. Yes. I believe it's a true vision of what's coming for our family in the future."

White Wolf murmured, "I hope it is so. It would be a wonderful gift to join our two races and families in a child. Perhaps it's time we invited Connal Lee to join our tipi. Wouldn't you agree, Short Rainbow? Screaming Eagle?"

Screaming Eagle answered by pulling them all together in a big hug, delighted by this turn of events. Short Rainbow whispered in Connal Lee's ear, "Yes. Please join our happy tipi."

The invitation thrilled Connal Lee. He hugged them back enthusiastically. In Shoshone, he eagerly agreed. "Yes. Please. I love each of you so much. I would love to call you my husbands and wife."

Short Rainbow chuckled. "Three husbands, and still only one wife to care for the tipi. We need to find more wives."

The following morning, as they rode north alongside the snow-topped Wasatch Mountain Range, Lorna broached the subject of the Shoshone family with Connal Lee. Connal Lee explained how they were now his husbands and wife. Lorna thought she should be shocked at the news but didn't find herself terribly surprised. She rode along quietly as she tried to imagine how the four of them made love and how they constituted a married family. She had trouble envisioning their love play at night. Who did what to whom and how? With three husbands, who took the role of the head of the household? Finally, she decided to just let it be. She couldn't do anything about it, anyway, at least not without offending one or all of the young family. That evening she observed the affectionate, caring way they all helped each other as they went about their various chores around the camp. She found herself approving their group relationship, despite herself.

Lorna whispered to Gilbert as they lay under their quilts in their little tent, "I'm shocked, yet I'm also pleased that Connal Lee has found love in his life."

Gilbert moaned sleepily. "Um-hm."

Traveling in slow stages to allow the Baines to become accustomed to riding, they grew close to the first permanent settlement by Europeans in the region, Fort Buenaventura. Miles Goodyear, a fur trapper and trader, had built it two years before the Mormons arrived. The tiny fort consisted of three log cabins, one for living, one for working, and one for fur storage. In the fourth corner stood an open-air workspace of a thatched roof held up on eight cedar posts. A ten-foot-tall stockade fence surrounded the Fort. Goodyear had built the entire stockade using old-fashioned mortise and tenon construction without a single nail. He had located the Fort on a broad plain between the Great Salt Lake to the west and craggy, snowcapped mountains to the east. Rivers and feeder creeks crossed the valley floor until they emptied into the lake, softening the desert with gray and green foliage. The fort's convenient location soon became known as Brownsville, then the City of Ogden a few years later.

Connal Lee returned from hunting with half a dozen grouse, each weighing around five pounds. Lorna and Short Rainbow worked together to fry them up in bacon grease after dipping them in cornmeal, salt, and dried sage. Lorna already had potatoes roasting in the fire's hot coals and ashes. After they finished eating, they sat in three couples with furs and quilts over their shoulders for warmth. Lorna cuddled up against Gilbert. "How much further is it to Fort Hall? Does anyone know?"

Screaming Eagle, who seldom spoke up during English conversations, nodded. "Around one hundred fifty mile more, Missus Baines. Around ten day at pace we travel."

Lorna sighed. "A little while yet, still. Well, it took us two weeks to travel south in the handcart company, so I shouldn't be surprised. Gilbert and I have been traveling for so long without a home. I'm yearning to put down roots and build a house. Plant a garden. Raise some chickens, goats, and pigs. I hope we can do that when we reach Fort Hall, don't you, Gilbert dear?"

Gilbert hugged her as he nodded his agreement.

That night White Wolf introduced Connal Lee to a loving way to share sex with another man. He carefully prepared Connal Lee's butt, licking and kissing it until it became well lubricated. He rolled Connal Lee over on his back, spread his legs, then slowly, carefully, tenderly inserted his strong erection in Connal Lee's clenching butthole. With a sigh of joy, White Wolf began gently thrusting. Short Rainbow and Screaming Eagle hugged their joined husbands, caressing their bodies as they made love. Connal Lee experienced the most intense orgasm of his life that night as White Wolf taught him new refinements in lovemaking. Connal Lee didn't want White Wolf to ever withdraw. When they calmed down, Screaming Eagle leaned over and whispered, "Ah, good. Now White Wolf has prepared the way for a real man to make love to you. Tomorrow, it's my turn!"

Connal Lee leaned over and hugged Screaming Eagle. "I love you, Screaming Eagle." Connal Lee turned over onto his back and gazed up at the constellation of Orion. *After all those times Paw penetrated me so painfully, Ah never expected to discover that sex in the behind could actually be pleasurable. It certainly never was with Paw, not even once. I wonder if Screaming Eagle's bigger man parts will also be as enjoyable. Ah can't wait to find out. Ah wonder what it feels like to enter another man's rear end. Ah hope Ah get to discover that soon, too.*

Their slow trip on horseback brought them to the Logan River. They camped at the same campsite they had used when traveling south with Chief SoYo'Cant. After seven more days of traveling cross country, they arrived at the big hot springs. They decided to take a day to rest and enjoy the natural heat, so welcome at the end of November.

That afternoon, Connal Lee shot a brace of big fat rabbits. Lorna put the meat to stewing in her big cook pot with plenty of potatoes, carrots, and onions. Short Rainbow and White Wolf used their metal blades to clean the skins of all meat and fat. Short Rainbow cooked up their brains and tanned the hides that evening. Lorna and Gilbert's English gloves had worn thin, so she stitched up two pairs of fur-lined riding gauntlets for them. When Short Rainbow handed Lorna the gloves, Lorna smiled and pulled them on. "Oh! Short Rainbow. These are so warm. Thank you, dear. Thank you." She watched with a smile as Gilbert pulled on his new riding gauntlets. "Thank you, my friends. These are just what we needed. Just perfect. Thank you ever so much."

The next day they woke up to find frost on the ground. The nighttime temperature had dropped below freezing. Clouds of steam rose from the hot springs, completely obscuring them from view.

Ten days after Connal Lee and his family left the hot springs, a small group of trappers, returning south from trading with Mr. Mackey, stopped to enjoy the springs. One of the men had developed a dry hacking cough during their trip to Fort Hall. His eyes watered. He sneezed a lot. They thought he had caught a cold. They lounged in the hot water, extolling its healing virtues, thinking it would help the sick trapper feel better. The mountain men took a last lingering bath the following morning before they went on their way. The sick trapper sneezed and spit into the springs as he repeatedly cleared his nose and throat, seeking relief from his worsening congestion.

By unfortunate coincidence, Chief SoYo'Cant led his tribe into the camp beside the hot springs early that same afternoon. Nearly everyone took advantage of bathing in the hot pools of water.

About eight days after Chief SoYo'Cant's clan returned to their winter camp, they began falling ill, running high fevers and coughing. Within four days of the onset of the fever, they started developing small grayish-white spots inside their mouths. Soon a reddish-brown rash broke out behind their ears before it spread over their bodies. Nearly half the camp had to stay in their sleeping furs for over a week. One in five did not survive the ravages of the high fever. Young and old, they died in every tipi, leaving the entire camp in mourning.

Chief SoYo'Cant later learned the white men called the disease measles. The Native Americans had no natural immunity against the highly contagious disease. It continued to spread through the camp until everyone had taken sick. Those who survived had natural immunity and would never catch the measles again.

Connal Lee and his Shoshone family rode north after leaving the hot springs. Four cold days later, their little party pulled up to Fort Hall. They stopped at the trading post in the fort and replenished their supplies. Connal Lee asked Mr. Mackey if he had heard any word from Captain Reed or Lieutenant Anderson. "Not since they accompanied the handcart company some weeks back, Connal Lee. You know, when White Wolf introduced you as Connal Lee, I thought Lee was your last name. I have already apologized to Zeff for my mistake. I hope you will forgive me, too. Zeff was so disappointed I didn't tell you he had staked a claim on the clay pit up north of here."

Before they left, Mr. Mackey gave them directions to Zeff's new homestead on the Snake River.

They spent that night camped outside the fort, down by the raging river. After a hot breakfast and cups of steaming coffee, they loaded up their horses and left for Zeff and Sister Woman's home. Later that morning, they spotted smoke rising ahead from beside the river. Excited to be reunited with his family, at last, Connal Lee kicked his fine mare in the stomach and raced ahead. He pulled up to the cliffside hovel, shouting, "Zeff! Sister Woman! It's me. Are y'all in there? Zeff! Sister Woman!"

When cold weather arrived, Zeff had built an unbaked adobe brick wall to close up the front of their cabin. Unpainted board shutters covered a small window to the left of the door. Suddenly, the narrow board door flung open. Zeff ran out the door, wearing a quilt as a shawl. "Baby Boy! Connal Lee! At last!"

They ran into each other's arms and hugged tightly. "Oh, how Ah've missed y'all, Baby Boy. At last, y'all have returned tuh the bosom o' yer family."

They pulled apart and looked each other in the eye. Their faces lit up in huge smiles. Sister Woman pulled on her warm wool coat and then rushed out to hug Connal Lee. Overwhelmed with joy, she broke down sobbing in his arms. Still smiling, Zeff pulled them both into a big warm hug. When Sister Woman calmed down, she complained, "We've been worried plumb tuh death, Connal Lee. Come on in an' tell us all about yerself. It's been months!"

They pulled Connal Lee into their dim little hut, lit and warmed only by a roaring fire in the cooking fireplace. They only owned two stick chairs Zeff had made. A rough mattress lay on the floor. Sister Woman had stitched it up and filled it with grass straw harvested from the desert. It barely made a thick quilt on the compacted dirt floor. Zeff gave Connal Lee a chair. Sister Woman sat on the mattress, legs crossed Indian style.

The arrival of Connal Lee's Shoshone family and foster parents interrupted their animated conversation. More hugs and shouted greetings ensued with a round of introductions. Zeff and Sister Woman fetched firewood and built a big bonfire in the stone-lined fire pit where they had pitched their tent when they first arrived. The Baines erected their little two-man tent not far from the firepit.

Zeff used his shovel to carry hot coals from their cookfire to light the campfire. A couple of young does hung cleaned and skinned from a tall cottonwood tree close by, nearly frozen through. Sister Woman and Short Rainbow cut venison steaks from one of them. Lorna fried the steaks for their supper.

They spent a festive, cold evening cooking and eating, laughing and crying, hugging and kissing.

Connal Lee kept gazing at Zeff, then Sister Woman, then little Chester Ray. The love and joy he felt infused his face with an angelic cast. He couldn't stop smiling, he felt so relieved and happy.

Lorna and Gilbert excused themselves with big yawns and went to their tent to sleep. Zeff invited Connal Lee to come inside and share their bed in the warmth of their one-room home. "Thanks, Zeff, but Ah'll sleep with my family here, like Ah'm used to now. Good night. See y'all in the morning."

Chapter 10: Fort Hall School

The roosters of Sister Woman's small flock of chickens awoke everyone at sunrise. Frost covered the ground. Shallow puddles of water along the river had frozen around their edges in thin, lacy patterns. Short Rainbow reluctantly pulled herself out of their warm bed. She dressed quickly, stirred up the fire, and added more cured pine logs from Zeff's woodpile. Sister Woman walked down to the fire carrying a pot of hot coffee to share. Zeff brought Chester Ray all swaddled up in his quilts for warmth.

While Lorna made pan bread, Connal Lee complained of the cold. Zeff nodded his head. "Yep. Mister Mackey told me he's never seen it git this cold this early. He said tuh take precautions fer a colder winter than usual, so Ah've been cuttin' extra firewood tuh get us ready."

Sister Woman walked back to her cellar home and returned carrying a shallow, unfired clay bowl full of speckled brown eggs and a tin plate holding slices of bacon. "Ah remembers how y'all tol' us ya like a big fry-up fer breakfast. Remember, back at Fort Laramie?"

Lorna's eyes opened wide in delight. "Oh, thank you, Sister Swinton. I do remember. Let me fry up everyone some bacon and eggs this morning, shall I? How wonderful!"

After they finished breakfast, Short Rainbow took charge of her husbands. "We need to raise my tipi today. I can't do it by myself."

Short Rainbow led the men closer to the river where they had parked the seven great travoises, still loaded with their goods. She selected three of the longest lodgepole pine trunks and handed one to Screaming Eagle and one to White Wolf. "Lay your poles on the ground, crossed at the top." She took a braided leather rope and tied the three poles together. Walking backward, she pulled the poles up into a giant tripod. "Spread out the base. Connal Lee, please come and hold my pole."

One by one, Short Rainbow raised more poles, leaning them against the tripod's top in an orderly fashion. Once she had a frame of poles, each evenly spaced three feet apart on the ground, Short Rainbow grabbed her leather rope and walked around the tipi frame four times, tying the tops together. She tied a smoke-blackened hide to one end of the last pole. "I'm going to need some help here. These hides are heavy."

Screaming Eagle helped her raise the leather covering to the top. Short Rainbow secured the lift pole in the last blank space, completing the circle. Short Rainbow swatted Screaming Eagle's arm in mock anger. "We need more wives! You husbands are wearing me out, both in bed and out. This family is too big for only one wife!"

In the way of husbands the world over, Screaming Eagle merely shrugged. "Yes, dear."

Connal Lee helped his family move their belongings into the tipi. He left two of his Crow sleeping blankets beside the bonfire for them to sit on. Lorna and Sister Woman worked together, making a hot stew for their midday meal. After eating, Zeff went into his hut and returned carrying two wrapped packages. He crossed his legs and sat down beside Connal Lee. He handed a book wrapped in brown paper to Connal Lee. "That nice Lieutenant Anderson brought y'all this book back when they came tuh escort us in tuh Fort Hall. He said it was 'is favorite book by Charles Dickens."

Even in his excitement, Connal Lee carefully untied the white butcher's string, unwrapped the paper, and set them aside to be reused later. He read the title on the leather binding and held the book up to show everyone. "Nicholas Nickleby. Ah can't wait to read it. Thanks, Zeff. Ah can't wait to see Lieutenant Anderson so Ah can thank him in person."

"Here, Connal Lee. Then yer important Captain Reed gave me this 'ere book fer ya. He said the canvas is waterproofed tuh keep yer book dry."

He handed Connal Lee the yellowed canvas package. Connal Lee unwrapped it carefully, noting how the ends tucked in to protect the book so he could rewrap it later. Reverently, he raised up the thick novel. "The Three Musketeers. Wow! Two books at one time. This is better than Christmas. Now we have something to read during the long winter evenings."

Connal Lee fanned the pages, thrilled to see all the words he had never read before. With a big grin on his face, he stood up and took the books and their wrappings into the tipi for safekeeping. When he returned to the fire, Zeff squeezed his knee. "The Captain said it's 'is favorite book about a young boy growin' up tuh be a soldier fer 'is king."

"That's so nice of my older brother to think of me. Don't y'all think so? Ah can't wait to see him so Ah can tell him how grateful Ah am to have his favorite book."

Lorna and Gilbert stood up. "Connal Lee, dear. Do you suppose we could borrow your horses this afternoon? We would like to ride over to the fort and learn more about the local community."

"Of course, Mother Baines. Let me help you saddle up. You know what? Ah think I'll go along with you. Does anyone else want to go with us?"

Zeff stood up. "Would y'all mind takin' some o' muh hides in tuh sell Mister Mackey?"

"Nope. Ah'll saddle up a packhorse."

A chilly hour later, they arrived at Fort Hall. They rushed through the door and pulled it closed to keep in the warmth. Mr. Mackey had a fire burning in a small potbelly stove. Lorna asked about what local community they had in the vicinity. Mr. Mackey told them about a small group of pioneers who had staked out their farmsteads a little north of the fort on the Blackfoot River, a tributary of the Snake River. He told them a few others were settling down a mile east of the fort along the north side of the Overland Trail. "What with the Shoshones being all peaceful like, they feel safe enough to stake their claims. We've built us a little schoolhouse here inside the Fort for all the children. It's a snug little two-room log cabin. One room for the classroom. The other room for the school teacher to live in. The problem is, we don't have a school teacher."

Lorna and Gilbert looked at each other. "Mister Mackey, I taught school back in Dunstable, England, before we immigrated. May I please see the schoolhouse?"

"Certainly, let me grab my coat. The schoolhouse is very close by." Fifteen minutes later, they returned to the warn trading post. Connal Lee traded Zeff's tanned furs for bags of dried fruits and beans. Lorna and Gilbert had their heads together, talking quietly. Connal Lee gazed around at the store overflowing with more trade goods than usual. He stepped over and inspected a small cook stove.

"Hey, Mister Mackey. Where did y'all get stoves way out here on the frontier? Look, Mother Baines, a stove with an oven. And what is this contraption, Mister Mackey?"

"Why, young man, that's a brand spanking new Singer sewing machine with a foot treadle."

"What? A machine to sew with? What will they think of next?"

"Yes, sir. It comes with boxes of needles and all kinds of threads on wooden spools. I read the pamphlet that came with it. Normally, Singer salespeople teach customers how to use their new sewing machines. The booklet claims this machine can even sew leather."

"Look, Mother Baines. Y'all enjoy sewing."

An hour later, they loaded up the packhorse with supplies. Connal Lee proudly strapped on two long narrow wooden boxes, two double-barreled shotguns for Screaming Eagle and White Wolf. He loaded on a heavy wooden crate of lead, buckshot, and gunpowder for Zeff.

As they rode home, Lorna thought out loud. "I think I could see ourselves living in that little schoolhouse, at least for this first winter here. If I bought a Singer sewing machine, I could sew up some rabbit skin gloves and mittens for sale. And if we bought a cookstove, I could bake bread and pastries and sell them to the men of the garrison. We could become independent right off. What would you think of that, Gilbert? What do you think, Connal Lee?"

"Sounds like a real good plan to me, Mother Baines. And Ah like the idea of y'all living so close to Zeff and Sister Woman. When Chief SoYo'Cant gets back to his winter camp down on the Portneuf River, Ah suspect we'll take Short Rainbow's tipi down and winter with the clan. Did Ah tell y'all that the great Chief SoYo'Cant, who the Mormons call Chief Arimo, adopted me as his son and a member of the Shoshone tribe?"

Lorna looked at him in amazement. "What is it about you, Connal Lee? Every time you turn around, you somehow manage to acquire more friends and family. First, you found two older foster brothers, the captain and the lieutenant. Then you adopted Gilbert and me as your foster parents. Then you adopted your little Shoshone family. And now an Indian Chief has adopted you. Everyone just loves you, son. You're amazing!"

"Ah don't do anything special. Ah just like everyone, is all."

Lorna shook her head in admiration.

That night, Connal Lee complained he didn't have candles or lamps so he could read his new novels after dark.

Lorna announced over breakfast, "Gilbert and I prayed about it last night. We also slept on it overnight to be certain we were not making a rash, impulsive decision. This morning we decided to go talk to Mister Mackey. I'll see if I can get that position and cabin as schoolmistress for the fort. Then, I'm going to put a deposit down on a sewing machine and a cookstove with an oven. Zeff, dear, would you please save all your rabbit skins for me to sew up into gloves and mittens? Sister Swinton, would you please teach us how to tan hides for ourselves?"

Screaming Eagle and White Wolf sat beside the fire, happily stripping and cleaning their new hunting rifles. Connal Lee noticed Short Rainbow eyeing the guns jealously. He decided he better buy her a rifle, too, to keep peace in the family. Even though he found the idea foreign to his concept of the proper roles for women, Connal Lee finally acknowledged Short Rainbow as a warrior and hunter. He realized the Shoshone didn't draw rigid lines between how men and women should live their lives the way Americans did. White women simply did not become soldiers or go to war. They had no option, even if they wanted to. Society wouldn't allow it. Connal Lee stood up. "Ah'll saddle up a horse for you, Mother Baines. Ah think Ah'll accompany you again today. Sister Woman, would you like any supplies from the post?"

It turned out that Short Rainbow and Sister Woman both wanted to go along. They all took off, leading a large packhorse with an empty packsaddle behind them.

Connal Lee thrilled Short Rainbow with her own brand new hunting rifle.

Mr. Mackey welcomed Lorna as the fort's new schoolmistress.

Connal Lee bought Lorna a sewing machine and cook stove. "Y'all can pay me back after your glove factory and bakery starts making money. No rush. Ah don't need much cash money living with my Shoshone family. We mostly hunt and make everything we need for living."

Lorna Baines gave Connal Lee an exuberant hug in thanks.

"When we head south for the Chief's camp, Ah'll leave two of the Crow horses behind so y'all have mounts. Things are too spread out here on the frontier for y'all to be without rides."

That evening while Short Rainbow broiled venison steaks with slices of liver, heart, and kidneys, she began rendering the deer's fat in a small cast iron pot at the edge of the fireplace. "What are y'all cooking, Short Rainbow? That looks like nothing more than fat or lard."

"Cook candle. Light at night for read."

"That sounds great! What do y'all use for a wick?"

Short Rainbow didn't know the English words, so she answered in Shoshone. "A cotton string is the best, but if I don't have any, I improvise by braiding the stems of the blue flax flower."

"What is blue flax?"

"I don't know. Go ask White Wolf or wait and ask Teniwaaten."

Short Rainbow tied together a large mug from the flexible bark of a white birch tree to form a mold for her tallow candle. Using fur mittens, she picked up the pot of rendered deer fat and carefully poured it into the mold. After it cooled, she unwrapped the mold and handed Connal Lee the candle. "Here. Light. Read."

"Thanks, Short Rainbow. This is great!"

That night Connal Lee began reading *The Three Musketeers* to his little family. They often stopped to explore the meanings of words his spouses didn't understand. They all enjoyed the entertainment. Finally, Connal Lee reluctantly closed the book, blew out the smelly candle, and crawled into their shared sleeping furs.

Connal Lee and Zeff taught Gilbert where to hunt rabbits and how to track them. Short Rainbow and Sister Woman tutored Lorna and Gilbert on how to skin, clean, and tan rabbit hides. When they learned how to prepare the skins both with and without the fur still attached, Lorna felt satisfied she could do it herself.

The Baines completed their preparations. Connal Lee helped Lorna and Gilbert move their meager belongings into the little log cabin in the schoolhouse. Mr. Mackey showed them how to set up a wood-burning cookstove since none of them had ever done it before.

He showed them how to install the tin chimney to vent the smoke out the side of the little one-room cabin.

While Connal Lee helped the Baines move, his Shoshone family cut down trees along the river bottom for firewood. After they replenished Zeff's woodpile, they borrowed his handcart. Using both the Swinton's and the Baines' handcarts, they transported firewood to the fort and stacked it next to the schoolhouse.

When they finished their chores, Lorna prepared a feast on her new cookstove. They ate in the classroom, delighted to be able to sit down together in a warm room to enjoy their supper. Over dessert and coffee, Connal Lee asked what he could take Chief SoYo'Cant as a gift when they returned to his winter camp. They couldn't think of anything. The Chief already had his own hunting rifle and Bowie knife. He didn't care for trinkets, beads, or white man food. Connal Lee ended up buying a gross of sharp steel hunting arrowheads for the Chief to distribute among his tribe as he saw fit.

Mr. Mackey told all his customers about Lorna's new bakeshop. "Take her a bag of flour. The next morning you can pick up bread or pastries made from half the flour. Missus Baines keeps the other half as payment for her other supplies, talents, and hard work. Her baked goods are so delicious they are worth the price, believe you me. How did we ever get along before she started her little bakery?"

Lorna soon had regular visitors dropping by her little cabin every day, placing orders for bread, rolls, cakes, and cookies. She became quite popular with the young privates stationed in the garrison. She soon knew most of them by name, especially those with a sweet tooth.

With everyone settling in for winter, White Wolf suggested they join Chief SoYo'Cant at his Portneuf River winter camp. As they ate supper, they agreed they would pack up the tipi and head south after breakfast in the morning.

Short Rainbow woke up just before dawn, perspiring heavily. She sat up with a start. White Wolf felt the blanket jerk away, which woke him up. The little fire had died low. The only light in the tipi came from a quarter moon shining dimly through the smoke hole at the top of the tipi. White Wolf reached for Short Rainbow and pulled her into a gentle hug. "What's wrong, Short Rainbow? Are you ill? Why are you shivering?"

Short Rainbow sat quietly for a moment with her head bowed. White Wolf reached for a rag of cotton cloth in a sweetgrass basket under the tipi's interior curtain wall. Gently he wiped her face and neck free of sweat. Short Rainbow leaned over close to White Wolf's ear. "I had a dream, a vision, I think, of trouble coming our way. It left me shaken. Then I heard the sound of an arrow hitting a body with a loud thud, and it startled me awake." She hesitated. White Wolf hugged her tighter as he eased her head down on his shoulder with gentle pats.

Screaming Eagle sensed something amiss and woke up. "Is everything all right? Why are you awake so early? It's not even dawn yet."

White Wolf softly replied, "Short Rainbow had a vision that disturbed her rest. Would you please stir up the fire? I don't think we'll be going back to sleep this morning."

Once the hot coals flared up, Connal Lee woke up to the flickering light and stretched. "Isn't this a little early to start for the Portneuf River? It's not even a full day's ride away."

Screaming Eagle added a few split logs to the little fire, then placed their coffee pot, filled with fresh river water the night before, close to the flames. White Wolf nodded his approval. "Good thinking, Screaming Eagle. Please find our dried spearmint leaves and brew a healing tea to start our day."

White Wolf crawled over and lifted the inner lining of the tipi. He retrieved a soft goatskin chamois and a dried gourd bowl, then filled the bowl with warm water from the coffee pot. He sat down beside Short Rainbow and began gently washing her face, neck, and breasts. He took his time and sent loving and calming thoughts through his hands. Connal Lee saw Short Rainbow's distress and wanted to help. He picked up a dry chamois and followed after White Wolf's healing hands, gently patting her dry. After they finished, Screaming Eagle shook out a soft rabbitskin blanket and wrapped it over Short Rainbow's shoulders. Screaming Eagle and Short Rainbow shared warm smiles.

They smelled the clean minty steam of the brewing tea. Connal Lee found the reed basket holding their drinking horns and served the tea. They sat silently, sipping tea, listening as the first birds greeted the dawn. Short Rainbow sat up taller and gazed around at her family. "I feel soiled by my vision, my dream. I feel tarnished in my soul, in my heart. White Wolf, would you please help me conduct a smudging ceremony and then build us a nasokokanrih? It would help me face whatever is coming if my body and spirit are cleansed and renewed before we carry on."

"Of course, Short Rainbow. We can all use a quiet time to renew ourselves spiritually."

Connal Lee hesitantly spoke up, not wanting to intrude on the quiet moment. "White Wolf, what is a nasokokanrih?" He stumbled on the long, strange word.

"Nasokokanrih translates in English to sweat lodge. I'll explain as we go, Connal Lee. A sweat lodge involves an ancient ceremony, simple but beautiful, about renewing our souls and being reborn clean and pure like an innocent baby. Screaming Eagle, let's go find the perfect spot to erect it. I think we should all fast this morning until we complete the purifications. Short Rainbow, perhaps you could find our dried lavender for the smudging ritual. We'll also need sweetgrass, juniper, and plenty of sage to clear away negative energy and bring harmony back into our lives."

Short Rainbow nodded. "I'll prepare everything, White Wolf. Thank you for doing this for me."

White Wolf, Screaming Eagle, and Connal Lee walked downriver, out of sight of Zeff's holding and Short Rainbow's tipi. Following a curve in the meandering river, they entered a small peninsula covered by grass, surrounded by bushes of willows and taller reeds. "Ah. Perfect. Don't you think, Screaming Eagle? We have mother earth under our feet, surrounded by the waters of life. Let's build the lodge here. Connal Lee, we will need a dozen or so lengths of rawhide strings, the herbs I asked Short Rainbow to gather, doeskins to cover the lodge, and coals to light the fire. Short Rainbow will know what we need. While you bring them, Screaming Eagle and I will dig the firepit and find stones to line it."

Connal Lee nodded. Without a word, he turned around and retraced their steps. When he entered the tipi, Short Rainbow asked him to let Zeff and Sister Woman know they would be gone for most of the day but would return to join them for supper. She didn't want them to come looking for them and disturb their spiritual journey.

Half an hour later, Connal Lee returned to the little peninsula carrying a small cast iron cookpot filled with hot coals. Short Rainbow and Connal Lee led packhorses carrying lovely woven baskets and bags full of herbs, rawhide strings, and drinking horns. The horses also had several soft doeskins to cover the lodge. Short Rainbow carried a small buffalo skin drum and drum beater, tied onto her back by a thin leather cord.

White Wolf stood facing the rising sun. He placed the hot coals on the ground before him and gestured for everyone to stand in a circle. He picked up a bound bunch of dried lavender about two inches thick and eighteen inches long. Holding it like a wand, he touched it to the coals until the tip began smoking with an aromatic perfume. He raised the wand to the east, then the south, the west, then the north. He lifted the lavender up to the creator in the sky, then down to mother earth. With a gentle smile, he stepped over to Short Rainbow. She closed her eyes and lifted her face up to the warm sun. White Wolf wafted smoke over her breasts, using his free hand to gently fan it up over her face. He slowly walked around her, smudging the smoke over her entire body. His meditations focused on the smoke carrying away all the bad energy and then dissipating in the clean air. He took his time and smudged Screaming Eagle and Connal Lee.

When he finished, Short Rainbow held out her hand. With her shaman training, she also knew the ritual. She took the short wand of lavender and smudged White Wolf on all sides. Her hand floated gracefully as she fanned the fragrant smoke over his body. When finished, she turned to the firepit for the sweat lodge. She repeated the salute to the six directions, then leaned down and purified the firepit with the last of the lavender smoke.

Moving with ritualistic care, White Wolf lifted the little pot of coals and carefully tipped a few into the openings in the tipi of twigs and branches over the firepit. He lit the fire's east gate, south gate, west gate, and north gate. The fire flared up. By the time it burned down and heated the large rocks filling the dugout firepit, they would have the lodge built over it.

White Wolf and Connal Lee cut down long willow branches. Screaming Eagle planted the thick ends into the ground in an oval pattern around the firepit. Short Rainbow bent the willows until they crossed about five feet above the grassy floor, then bound them with rawhide strings. They worked out from the tallest central arch and created two smaller arches to the east and west. Finally, they made a low arch, barely thirty inches tall, to be their doorway on the eastern side.

White Wolf would have preferred white sage to cover the floor, but it only grew in the spring and summer. White Wolf asked Connal Lee to help him harvest willow leaves, most of which had turned yellow or red in the frost. They covered the grassy floor with fresh, clean-smelling leaves. Satisfied, White Wolf sprinkled dried white sage leaves over the willow leaves to purify them. The fire had burned down to coals, leaving the large rocks lining the firepit heated through.

White Wolf stepped back and placed his arm over Connal Lee's shoulder. "See? The oval shape of the sweat lodge symbolizes an expectant mother resting against mother earth, gazing up at the creator in the blue skies above. Her belly, so full of life, pushes upwards, like the shape of the lodge."

They watched Short Rainbow and Screaming Eagle work in tandem, covering the lodge. "As you duck down to crawl into the dark interior of the lodge, think of it as entering mother earth's womb, just as you were as a child growing in your mother's womb. When you crawl inside, move to your right. Be careful to avoid touching the hot stones in the center. Take a seat against the wall. I'll be today's lodge man and sit on the far west side. You may not understand all the words, chants, and rituals, so let me briefly explain. We will go through four rounds of prayer ceremonies. The first honors our ancestors and the Creator. We will pray for the well-being of our grandparents and their grandparents. Then I will sprinkle medicine water on the hot rocks to release the Creator's breath in the steam. The steam will make you sweat, pushing everything negative out of your body and soul.

"The second ceremony will be a prayer for our families and all the animals who give us life. We will pray for the two-legged and four-legged beasts and all living creatures with fins and wings. Again, I will sprinkle medicine water on the hot stones to make more steam.

"The third prayer will be for Short Rainbow, that her heart will be purified and filled with strength to help her with her upcoming trials. After more steam, while breathing the Creator's breath, we will begin the fourth prayer asking for help to overcome our personal weaknesses and shortcomings, for help in becoming the best we can possibly be."

Connal Lee nodded that he understood, though his mind brimmed over with questions. White Wolf stood up and began carefully placing his garments to the side. The others followed his lead. White Wolf picked up the drum, bowed down to his hands and knees beside the low portal, and pushed through the leather curtain. "It is time to enter the womb."

White Wolf crawled inside. Connal Lee followed next, then Screaming Eagle and Short Rainbow. Connal Lee sat beside White Wolf. Once the curtain closed over the opening, he couldn't see anything.

White Wolf began beating the drum in a soft, steady, throbbing rhythm. After a few minutes, the drum seemed to become a shared heartbeat, like a mother's heartbeat heard by a child in the womb. Connal Lee found his breathing slowing down to match the beat. He closed his eyes, but it made no difference in the absolute dark. White Wolf chanted the ritual's words. Short Rainbow added her voice. The drum never broke its rhythm.

After a few moments of silence, except for the constant drumbeat, Connal Lee jerked back when he heard a hiss of steam. A fragrant heat rose up around him. He breathed in deeply, smelling the perfumes of sweetgrass, white sage, and the piney aroma of cedar. His muscles began relaxing from the heat like in the hot springs.

When White Wolf began praying for the people and beasts in their lives, Connal Lee found his head nodding in time with the heartbeat drumming. With the next burst of hot steam, he felt sweat dripping off his forehead and trickling down his ribs. His head dropped forward until his chin rested on his chest.

White Wolf and Short Rainbow chanted the third prayer as the lodge became hotter, praying for Short Rainbow's health and strength in the face of adversity. Another burst of fragrant steam. Connal Lee became light-headed and dreamy as if half asleep. The drumming continued. Connal Lee became aware of White Wolf whispering, "Give thanks to Mother Earth that you are alive. Take joy in being alive this glorious day."

The drumming slowed down. Connal Lee felt drowsy. His mind wandered as he remembered falling in love with his wife and brother husbands. He felt nearly overcome as a peaceful joy welled up in his breast. He heard a louder final beat on the drum, then White Wolf softly proclaimed, "It is time to be reborn."

Screaming Eagle, closest to the portal, crawled out first. He held the doeskin curtain aside while his spouses crawled out. Connal Lee felt humbled and peaceful as he crawled through and stood up. He swayed slightly, but Screaming Eagle's strong hand held him steady. Connal Lee reached out and helped Short Rainbow rise gracefully to her feet. They smiled at each other and hugged. White Wolf pushed through the leather curtain, placed the drum aside, and rose to his feet. He looked Short Rainbow in the eye and nodded with a peaceful smile.

With their emotions running high, they communicated without words, hugging, kissing, smiling, and gazing deeply into each other's eyes. White Wolf picked up the small basket of drinking horns and led his family to the river bank. They leaned over and splashed water on their hot faces, arms, and torsos, then drank the clean, ice-cold water. Refreshed, they returned to the lodge and pulled on their clothing. Although the day had turned sunny and cool, they remained over-heated from the sweat lodge. They sat down on the grassy field and lounged in each other's arms as they cooled off and returned to the natural world. They savored the warm sun overhead and the fresh air moving over them in a gentle breeze.

Without speaking, they removed the lodge's covering and packed up. Holding hands, they took their time walking upstream to Zeff and Sister Woman's home.

The following day, they dismantled the tipi. After saying their goodbyes, they traveled south along the Snake River. Connal Lee thought about his participation in the sweat lodge as he rode with his family. He didn't understand the ceremonies and chanting but had found the experience more than a little interesting. Somehow he still felt cleansed and renewed, inside and out, though he couldn't explain the whys or hows of it.

When they arrived at Chief SoYo'Cant's camp, Short Rainbow and her sisters raised the tipi. Connal Lee suggested they visit the chief's campfire and let him know they had returned. They found the chief holding a council of war with Chief Pocatello and some of his warriors about Colonel Johnston and his heavily armed army of two-thousand five-hundred white foot soldiers. Chief Pocatello became enraged when he heard their sacred Shoshone lands would be invaded by so many armed men, a serious threat to the Shoshone Nation of nine thousand men, women, and children. The Shoshone would be hard-pressed to raise even a thousand armed and trained warriors to defend their people. They only owned a handful of rifles and pistols in all the clans, leaving them seriously outgunned.

Connal Lee, White Wolf, and Screaming Eagle strode up to the fire. Chief SoYo'Cant stood up and greeted his family with smiles and hugs. Young Arimo rose to his feet to welcome his adopted brother. When Pocatello observed SoYo'Cant hugging a blond, blue-eyed white boy, he jumped to his feet, infuriated. He pulled out a big flint hunting knife and started towards Connal Lee. Connal Lee glanced up and saw Pocatello rushing toward him threateningly. He pulled back in surprise. Chief SoYo'Cant turned around. When he saw Pocatello approaching, knife in hand, he interposed himself in front of Connal Lee with his arms held out wide. White Wolf and Screaming Eagle pulled their Bowie knives and moved beside their chieftain. Arimo pulled his volcanic glass knife out of its beaded sheath and stood beside White Wolf in a fighter's crouch with his blade held at the ready.

The Chief raised his hand, palm out. "Stop, Chief Pocatello. This is my adopted son, Connal Lee Swinton. To harm him is to harm my family and make me an enemy for life."

Two of Pocatello's warriors stood up and closed ranks with their chief with their knives drawn, ready to rid the earth of another despised pale face intruder. Chief Pocatello screamed, "Why do you have a white boy living in your camp? We must exterminate all white vermin before they infest our sacred hunting grounds. How can you even abide looking at his ugly pale skin, anyway? It's disgusting!"

To Pocatello's astonishment, Connal Lee stepped calmly over beside Screaming Eagle and looked Pocatello directly in the eye. Slowly, he raised his hand in the sign of Peace. In very clear Shoshone, he called out, "Peace, Chief Pocatello. Chief SoYo'Cant adopted me into his family, clan, and tribe. I presently share the tipi of the chief's niece, Short Rainbow, and with Screaming Eagle, here, and with White Wolf. I greet you in peace."

Chief Pocatello stared in amazement at hearing Connal Lee speaking his language. Pocatello's eyes squinted in a glare of pure hatred. Finally, after staring at Connal Lee standing so calmly and confidently beside Screaming Eagle, he threw up his hands, angry and frustrated. He spun on his toes and stamped out of Chief SoYo'Cant's open-air council lodge. His men formed up behind him and marched away, frowning and scowling hatefully at Connal Lee.

After Chief Pocatello's men disappeared behind a tent, everyone sighed a collective sigh of relief that no violence had resulted from the intense confrontation. Chief SoYo'Cant waved his hand towards the space they had just vacated. "Please, everyone, have a seat. Welcome back to my winter camp. Connal Lee, my son, I apologize on behalf of my fellow chieftain. I know he always advocates war against the white man, but I didn't think he would threaten you in my presence. Usually, he has better manners and exercises more self-control."

Connal Lee nodded respectfully. "Aeshen. Thank you, Father SoYo'Cant. It good be back your fire."

Everyone sat down. Quiet descended over the small group sitting around the large fire while they reflected on the tense scene they had just witnessed. Three of the chief's young nieces arrived with drinking horns of hot wild rosehip tea. The Chief told Connal Lee about his discussions and councils with the leaders of the various clans of the Shoshone, Bannock, and Blackfoot tribes. They were all trying to figure out the best way to deal with the Federal Army and still maintain the peace with their Mormon neighbors.

Connal Lee translated the ancient proverb into Shoshone and told Chief SoYo'Cant, "Enemy of friend is my enemy. I read in Bible while cross great plain."

Chief SoYo'Cant nodded his head in agreement. "Just so, son. Just so."

Short Rainbow's youngest sister walked up to White Wolf and whispered in his ear, "Short Rainbow asked me to tell you we have finished raising her tipi. It's safe for you to come back to her camp as all the work is done now. Besides, she has supper ready."

White Wolf whispered back, "Thank you, Bright Star." He stood up and held out his hand to Connal Lee. "Let's go eat supper."

They said goodbye to the chief and walked towards the northern edge of the sprawling camp where Short Rainbow had pitched her tipi.

Later that night, the first people in the camp began running fevers. Within days, nearly half the clan had become sick. Those who were not ill tended those that were, which exposed them to the invisible virus that caused measles. Connal Lee and his family helped White Wolf and Short Rainbow minister to the ill as best they could. None of them had any experience with this new illness. White Wolf and Short Rainbow met in consultation with Firewalker and Burning Fire, trying to deduce the best courses of action to help cure the sick and protect their people. They decided they could only keep everyone clean and warm. They prescribed willow bark and sage teas for everyone, sick or not.

Burning Fire meditated herself into a trance but received no inspiration or guidance from the spirit world about how to counter this new white man threat.

As they ate supper in the warmth of the tipi, Short Rainbow mused aloud. "It's clear now. This evil sickness is the arrow I heard strike a body dead in my vision the night before we built the sweat lodge. If only it were just one arrow and one death, not so many. So very many."

Connal Lee snuggled up to Screaming Eagle's broad back. He had nearly fallen asleep when he heard voices raised in mournful wailing from a neighboring tipi. A few minutes later, it subsided into sobbing. He knew another clan member had begun his journey to the happy hunting ground.

About ten days after the onset of the outbreak, Screaming Eagle, White Wolf, and Short Rainbow awoke running very high fevers. Connal Lee didn't know, but he had survived a bout of measles as an infant, which made him immune. He couldn't catch the measles again. Frantic with worry, he tended to his spouses, feeding them teas and broths until the sores in their mouths hurt too much to drink anything but plain water. Lovingly, Connal Lee bathed their feverish bodies, praying they would recover. His patients started sweating from the fever ravishing their systems. Through his raspy sore throat, White Wolf instructed Connal Lee to help them drink plenty of water so they wouldn't become dehydrated and start shriveling from lack of fluids. Seeing his loved ones in such a weakened condition, Connal Lee grew increasingly frightened of being left alone.

Short Rainbow's youngest sister, Bright Star, visited Short Rainbow's tipi the next day. Through sobs of sorrow, she informed Short Rainbow that their grandmother, who had raised them, had passed away during the night. Short Rainbow began crying, devastated at the sad news. Bright Star leaned down and gave Short Rainbow a brief hug before she hurried back to help their mother, who remained seriously ill in her own tipi.

Because of the small population of the winter camp, once the measles virus had infected everyone, it died out.

A long stressful week later, Connal Lee's three spouses began feeling better, though the fever left them weak and aching in their joints. Connal Lee began feeding them solid foods again in soups and stews. Finally, they began recovering and sitting up. In the quiet evenings of the mourning camp, he read them *The Three Musketeers* for a second time. They all enjoyed the adventures of d'Artagnan in Paris, fighting duels, outsmarting Cardinal Richelieu, defending the Queen's honor, and making friends with Athos, Aramis, and Porthos.

When everyone returned to normal, they helped Short Rainbow visit the survivors as she ministered to their sorrows and grief. Chief

SoYo'Cant and his first wife, White Dove, had survived, though his second wife and several other members of the chief's large family had not.

The chief and his son, Arimo, walked the camp, offering comfort and encouragement to his despondent, mourning clan. When Chief SoYo'Cant found families where both parents had died, he arranged for the grandparents or aunts and uncles to adopt the orphans. Where he found tipis where the husband had died, he helped the wives merge with the families of other loved ones so life could go on. Everyone felt shaken at the losses in every tipi to this new evil in their lives. The clan's population fell by a full twenty percent, without respect to age or gender.

After the weather turned much colder, Connal Lee's family developed new routines. Short Rainbow and White Wolf spent their mornings at those daily chores that provided their living. They tanned leather and sewed warm furs into cloaks to wear over their coats like big capes. They made arrows and cast lead bullets. They dried and processed the last of the herbs they had harvested for food and medicines.

Screaming Eagle and Connal Lee walked outside the camp and practiced shooting bows and rifles every day. Screaming Eagle began teaching Connal Lee how to fight with knives. Connal Lee practiced throwing knives every day until he could send the knifepoint straight into a target to kill him or accurately throw the handle at a target to incapacitate someone without killing them.

Every day, the four spouses paused to take their cold noon meal together, thankful they were all still alive after being so deathly ill. After they ate, White Wolf went to study with Firewalker, and Short Rainbow left to study with Burning Fire. When Teniwaaten had time free from teaching the clan's children, Connal Lee practiced the Shoshone language with him. Usually, he accompanied Screaming Eagle down to the river basin bottomlands to hunt. They hunted to feed their family and obtain hides for clothing and trade.

By the middle of December, the temperature never rose above freezing. Two days later, they had their first snowfall. Nearly two feet of dry, smooth, powdery snow covered everything for as far as the eye could see. Somehow the soft snow muffled almost all sounds. Their world became quiet and still. The horses had to kick away the snow to reach the dried fodder around the camp. This forced them to forage further and further away as they searched for food. The camp became even quieter as many of the wives and children stayed in their tipis warmed by fires as they did their chores. Many families let in a few of their favorite dogs to entertain the youngsters in the warmth.

Shortly after the first snow, Zeff surprised Connal Lee when he rode down to Chief SoYo'Cant's camp, his first time ever to visit. Three of the camp's warriors saw him approaching and rode out to intercept him. Zeff held up his hand with his elbow bent. "Peace."

The guards returned the greeting and escorted him to Chief SoYo'Cant's fireplace in the big cold outdoor lodge. A large bonfire burned briskly before the open-faced council chamber. Zeff and the Chief introduced themselves. Zeff asked if he could please see Connal Lee and his Shoshone family. One of the Chief's young nephews took Zeff by his gloved hand and led him to Short Rainbow's tipi.

Short Rainbow welcomed him and invited him in. After joyful greetings all around, Zeff shared the news that Captain Reed and Lieutenant Anderson were on their way to Fort Hall, accompanying an army convoy of wagons full of supplies. Some of the cavalrymen would remain behind to reinforce the garrison at the Fort. Others would ride back to Fort Laramie, patrolling and guarding the trail on their way. The remainder would ride west to Oregon and California, ensuring the security of the trail. News of the restlessness of the natives, mainly due to Colonel Johnston's army heading their way, had reached Major Sanderson in Fort Laramie. While the cavalry normally wouldn't undertake an expedition in the cold of winter, the Major didn't think they should wait until spring. He took the possibility of an uprising and violence against white travelers and settlers very seriously.

The Major also sent the small garrison at Fort Hall a combination gristmill and sawmill. He ordered the Fort's soldiers to expand its barracks, horse barns, and storerooms. They had to accommodate a permanent addition to the garrison of fifty new cavalrymen and all their horses and supplies.

Captain Reed had sent a messenger ahead of the wagon train so Fort Hall would be ready to receive the large convoy and new troops. Zeff didn't know, so he couldn't have told Connal Lee, but the Captain had ordered the commanding officer's quarters cleared out so he would have a place to stay when he arrived. He advised the Lieutenant in charge of the small military garrison in Fort Hall that he had purchased a Conestoga wagon and oxen team to transport all his own furniture, bedding, and provisions to his new post.

Connal Lee felt thrilled to hear his cavalry heroes would arrive in only three days.

That evening over supper in Short Rainbow's tipi, Connal Lee asked his family to help him locate four large buffalo hides. He wanted to make sleeping furs for his older foster brothers, Captain Reed and Lieutenant Anderson, to repay them for their friendship and wonderful gifts of two fine novels. Everyone agreed that would be a great way to welcome them to the Fort.

After breakfast the following morning, Connal Lee invited Zeff to meet him at Fort Hall in three days. "Unless something comes up, we'll join y'all, Little Brover."

"Have a safe journey home, Big Brover. Thanks for taking the time to bring me this great news. Give my love to Sister Woman and Mother and Father Baines, will you, please?"

"Ah will. Bye, now, Connal Lee. See y'all in a coupla days!"

Chapter 11: Cavalry Family

Connal Lee's Shoshone family helped him find four dark brown buffalo hides, averaging seven feet long and five feet wide. The heavy fur varied in length up to five inches along the spine. While Screaming Eagle and White Wolf hunted, Short Rainbow showed Connal Lee how to trim the edges of the tanned hides into blankets. They ran out of time to decorate the skin sides, but Connal Lee thought they looked beautiful without any adornment.

Short Rainbow stitched up four hats from muskrat skins in her free time. Each fur-lined hat had flaps that could be tied up on the sides or lowered to cover the ears and tied under the chin. Connal Lee loved the light brown color of the soft fur. Screaming Eagle enjoyed the warmth of his new hat but missed wearing his proud war bonnet.

The day after Zeff returned back north, Short Rainbow invited her older and younger sisters to help her dismantle and pack up her tipi. They would need it for warmth when they visited Fort Hall. They worked as a team, having practiced together many times between their grandmother's tipi, their mother's tipi, and Short Rainbow's tipi. Short Rainbow stood working beside her youngest sister, Bright Star. Bright Star leaned over a few minutes later and whispered, "Guess what, Short Rainbow?"

Short Rainbow stopped and looked at her little sister's radiant face with a smile. "What, Bright Star?"

"I have grown up these past two months. I am now a woman. Mother suggests I leave her tipi, now that I have started my monthly courses, so I can spread my wings and mature and develop even more with other people and gain new experiences. Aren't you happy for me?"

"Oh, Bright Star! That is wonderful news. My little sister all grown up!" They stopped working long enough for Short Rainbow to pull Bright Star in for a congratulatory hug. "And you've grown up so lovely, too. So beautiful. I'm really very happy for you."

"Thank you." Bright Star turned back to her work before she hesitated. Coyly, she looked over at Short Rainbow, shy at being so outspoken about womanly matters. "Um, Short Rainbow? I have heard you complain many times this past year about needing someone to help care for your tipi and your husbands."

Short Rainbow turned back around and looked her little sister in the eye. "Yes. That's true. We have been hoping to find a second wife, but it hasn't happened yet."

"Well, might I accompany you when you leave this time? I will work very hard and help you out in every way. Please? May I come live and travel with you for a while? Please?"

"We all work very hard, Bright Star. It won't be easy like living in grandmother's tipi as a young girl."

"I can work hard, Short Rainbow. I'm strong. Let me prove it to you. After all, I am all grown up, now."

"Do you speak any English? With Connal Lee sharing my tipi, we converse more and more in English so we can all improve our vocabularies. We also spend time each day practicing Shoshone with Connal Lee so he can become more fluent."

"Well, Teniwaaten has been teaching me English these past four years along with the other children. I don't know if I'm up to having a conversation in English, but I understand a lot of what I hear. It's easier for me to hear English than to speak it. I would be happy to work on improving my English even more if only you would take me with you. Please? Please?"

"Do you know how to cook? Do you hunt and tan leathers?"

"I've been helping grandmother prepare meals for the past several years. I confess, I'm not a good hunter, but I have had a lot of experience in butchering, tanning, and sewing."

"Well, that's no matter. Hunting is something we can easily teach you." Short Rainbow hesitated. She looked away as she softly asked, "Do you have any experience in making love?"

Bright Star looked shyly down at the ground. A blush rose up her cheeks. "Not really, big sister. I have played childish games with some of the boys and girls, but we mostly only kissed and teased each other's bodies in innocent ways."

Short Rainbow pulled Bright Star into her arms once again. *So innocent. Still a virgin with so much of life still ahead of her. Am I patient enough to teach her? We've always liked each other. I think she could be good company for my family. She's so lively, so lovely, so delicate. Her beauty and innocence will enchant my rough and lusty husbands. Oh my, yes.*

Short Rainbow backed out of their tender hug and smiled at Bright Star. "Let me go find my lazy husbands who are avoiding work while we dismantle my tipi. Let me discuss it with them. I suspect they will be happy to give it a try. I only hope they won't be too much for you. Three bold men against one innocent young girl."

"Oh, thank you, Short Rainbow. I won't disappoint you. I will obey you as first wife, always. Let me try. With any luck, we will all come to love each other as we get to know each other." She stopped and lowered her eyes, suddenly shy again. "Besides, I confess I find all three of your husbands very handsome, very attractive each in their own way. I would so love to get to know them better."

"Well, keep working on the tipi. I'll be back as soon as I can."

About half an hour later, Short Rainbow skipped over to the bare poles of her tipi, dragging Screaming Eagle and Connal Lee along by their hands. White Wolf dogged their heels, grinning foolishly. Bright Star's lithe figure and glorious smile had enchanted him as he watched her grow up. White Wolf had fantasized more than once about enticing her to his blankets after she matured. It filled him with delighted anticipation when he heard she had become a woman.

Bright Star glanced up from tying a buffalo hide onto a travois. When she saw Short Rainbow leading her husbands toward her, she jumped up. Her face lit up with joy. She could tell from their expressions they had already agreed to let her travel with them.

"Connal Lee, this is my youngest sister, Bright Star. You've seen her around, but I don't think you were ever introduced. Bright Star, this is my third husband and our adopted cousin, Connal Lee Swinton."

Bright Star blushed before she remembered the white man manners learned from Teniwaaten. She held out her hand for a handshake. Connal Lee studied her pretty face, glowing like her name, as she delicately shook his hand. She shared the same pixyish beauty as Short Rainbow's, clearly her sister. "How do you do, Bright Star? I'm very pleased to meet y'all."

"I well, Connal Lee. Thank you. How do you do?"

They stood there looking each other over. Impatient, White Wolf pulled Bright Star into a welcoming hug. He nuzzled up under her ear. "I'm so happy you will be helping Short Rainbow this trip. This is a most wonderful development."

Screaming Eagle joyfully embraced White Wolf and Bright Star in his strong arms. "Welcome to our little family, Bright Star. I hope you will like us."

With a giggle, Bright Star twittered, "I already do. Thank you for letting me travel with you."

Amused at her randy husbands' obvious delight, Short Rainbow turned to business. "Well, Bright Star, you better go get packed up. Do you need horses? I can lend you some if you do."

"Oh, thank you, Short Rainbow. I have a pretty mare of my own I like to ride, but I don't own any packhorses. Can I borrow two for my clothing and blankets? Oh, I'm so excited. Thank you for letting me go with you, everyone. Thank you!"

With a new skip in her step, she bounced off to organize and pack her belongings.

The three warriors rode their favorite great war horses. Connal Lee rode his favorite brown mare. Bright Star rode a high-stepping palomino mare that matched her joyful temperament. They each led packhorses with plenty of food, the buffalo blankets for Connal Lee's cavalry brothers, and furs for trading. Short Rainbow's great draft horses pulling her tipi on four big travoises brought up the rear. Since they wouldn't be staying long at Fort Hall, they left most of their stores of food, tools, and other possessions in the Portneuf River camp until their return. They took their time and arrived at the fort shortly after midday.

Connal Lee asked everyone to relax a moment while he found out where the army would be setting up their tent camp. Connal Lee rushed into the trading post. "Hi, Mister Mackey. How are y'all doing this fine day?"

"I'm well, Connal Lee. How are you? What's this? You arrive without furs?"

"Oh, don't worry. We brought some really nice pelts for you. But first, do y'all happen to know where the army plans on setting up their tent camp when they arrive? We brought Short Rainbow's tipi and want to pitch it close to where Captain Reed's tent will be placed."

Mr. Mackey nodded his head. "I heard the soldiers talking about setting up everyone on the west side of the Fort as close as possible to fresh water from the river."

"Oh, good. Let me go get us organized and set up our camp. Ah'll come back and bring our furs later."

"See you later, then."

Connal Lee led his family around the corner from the gate in the south side of the domineering whitewashed fort. They worked as a team and raised the tall tipi. Along their way, they had gathered dead-fall for their fires. Short Rainbow and Bright Star built a stone-lined fire pit in the tipi, slightly off-center towards the entrance.

Connal Lee tied a small frying pan onto the packhorse carrying their trade furs and led the horse to the trading post. While Mr. Mackey totaled up the value of the tanned pelts, Connal Lee browsed the store. He noticed a used four-man army tent. He thought it would be a good idea to have a tent his family could use when they visited the fort. It required too much time and effort to carry Short Rainbow's tipi for short visits. This way, they could sleep out of the weather. He traded furs for the tent and took the balanced owed in cash. He loaded the tent onto the packhorse and then carried the frying pan back inside. "Could we borrow a few coals to light our fire, Mister Mackey?"

Mr. Mackey nodded his consent and waved Connal Lee over to his little potbelly heat stove.

While Connal Lee traded in the fort, Screaming Eagle took a packhorse and rode northwest, searching for fresh game for their supper. On his way towards the river, he ran into Zeff and his family, traveling down to the fort. They stopped and spoke briefly. Screaming Eagle told Zeff he could find Connal Lee at Short Rainbow's tipi on the west side of the fort.

Connal Lee rushed in and lit Bright Star's fire. He had spotted Zeff and his mule-drawn handcart approaching, so he went outside to greet them. After hugs and kissing little Chester Ray's forehead, he invited everyone to come in and warm up. Connal Lee introduced

Bright Star, then told everyone about buying a used tent. He turned to Zeff and Sister Woman. "Would y'all like to use it tonight?"

Zeff and Sister Woman looked at each other and nodded their heads.

"Well, come on then, let's get it pitched right next to our tipi."

While they worked at erecting the tent, Connal Lee winked at White Wolf. "Let's take a lesson from our native friends and place the door facing east away from the prevailing winds. That will help keep it warmer inside."

The tent's door ended up facing the whitewashed wall of the fort. White Wolf and Short Rainbow admired the tent and the simplicity of setting it up. They both approved of having a smaller tent for visiting the fort.

After they finished erecting the tent, Zeff and Sister Woman unpacked their quilts and baby clothes. Sister Woman carried Chester Ray back to Short Rainbow's warm tipi. Zeff took the mule-drawn handcart, still loaded with furs, over to the trading post and traded the tanned hides for more supplies and tools.

Mr. Mackey informed Zeff that Captain Reed would need to place a large order of bricks to build the foundation of a new watermill. "The windmill will power saws for cutting lumber and turn gristmills for grinding flour. Won't that be something?"

Zeff felt thrilled to hear about the big upcoming order. "Ah thanks y'all fer givin' me a heads up, Mister Mackey. This's really great news!"

Zeff loaded his purchases on his handcart and then led the draft mule fifty feet further along to the new school building. He stopped in front of Lorna's cabin and knocked. Lorna opened the door. "How nice to see you, Zeff. Please come in."

"Howdy, Sister Baines. Please wait a minute. Ah brung y'all somethin'."

Zeff lifted three burlap-wrapped bundles out of the cart and placed them on Lorna's rough little table. He then carried in a bale of tanned rabbit skins tied with a rawhide string.

"What on earth, Zeff? What is all this?"

"Well, now, a coupla weeks ago, Sister Woman asked me tuh bake 'er up some plates. Ah worked out a mixture close tuh like stoneware an' fired 'em up. Ah used a simple ash glaze from the local cottonwood trees."

Zeff unwrapped one of the round bundles. He lifted up a speckled beige dinner plate and showed it to Lorna. "They turned out right nice, don't y'all think? When we was done, Sister Woman helped me make up a set fer y'all. Merry Christmas, Sister Baines. We hopes y'all likes 'em."

"This is a princely gift, Zeff! My thanks to both of you. Dishes cost way too much at the trading post. I really appreciate this, Zeff. So thoughtful. I will use these for supper tonight. And thank you for the rabbit skins. Now I can start practicing with the treadle sewing machine in earnest."

A knock on the door interrupted their conversation. Lorna opened it. "Ah, Private Jackson. Please come in. I have your bread cooling right here."

She handed the private a golden brown loaf of freshly baked bread and three dozen sugar cookies wrapped in a scrap of a flour sack. "Oh, thank you, ma'am. Smells right heavenly, they do. Good night, now, ma'am."

After setting up the camps, White Wolf and Connal Lee rode southwest to the river basin to find deadfall and chop down firewood for their stay. They each led a packhorse to carry the wood. They didn't like burning green wood, but they would have no choice if they didn't find enough deadfall. Short Rainbow and Bright Star built a ring of heavy river rocks to contain their cookfire between her tipi door hole and the fort's wall.

An hour later, Connal Lee and White Wolf returned to their new camps. They unloaded the wood, and a large doe White Wolf had shot, then joined Zeff's family in the warm tipi. A little while later, Lorna and Gilbert arrived. Short Rainbow stood up to welcome them. "Please come Missus Baines, Mister Baines." She reached down and lifted up Bright Star by her hand. "I introduce little sister. She Bright Star in English. Bright Star, these adopted parents Connal Lee."

Bright Star danced over to shake hands. "How do you do? How do you do?"

Lorna held Bright Star's hand for a moment with a welcoming smile. "I'm doing very well, thank you, Bright Star. Such a pleasure to meet you. I can see a definite family resemblance. You and your sister are both so lovely."

Bright Star looked at Connal Lee for an interpretation. When he finished, she beamed a big smile. "Nice meet. Nice meet."

They all sat down around the warm fire, catching up and making plans. Lorna invited everyone to join her for supper in her classroom, where she had a heat stove, rustic tables, and chairs. "I started some bread dough to rising this morning before class. I'll go finish kneading it and bake us some rolls for supper. Shall we plan on eating at sunset, then?"

As Lorna and Gilbert were leaving, Screaming Eagle arrived with four fat grouse.

While Short Rainbow, Bright Star, Sister Woman, and Lorna cooked a communal supper, Connal Lee and White Wolf walked back to the trading post leading two packhorses laden with furs. They walked in to find Mr. Mackey reading The Weekly Missouri Democrat at his big work table. It was barely three weeks old. "Hello, again, Connal Lee. Good afternoon, White Wolf." Mr. Mackey folded up the newspaper and set it aside, shaking his head sorrowfully with a big sigh.

Connal Lee noticed the look on his face. "Why, whatever is the matter, Mister Mackey? What's the news from back east?"

"Oh, I just finished reading last month's newspaper from Saint Louis. It appears we're having another influenza epidemic, not just in Missouri but all across the nation. In fact, the paper reported it has already spread all around the world. It's pretty serious this year, apparently as bad as the eighteen forty-seven worldwide epidemic we all lived through. Nearly ten percent of those who come down with the flu this winter aren't surviving it. Terrible. Just terrible. It appears that pretty much everyone is coming down with it, even if they've had the flu before. It's creating chaos as the world's local and national governments struggle to cope with the sick, the dying, and the dead. Patients are lining the floors of the halls of the hospitals, waiting for beds in Saint Louis. The mortuaries are swamped. They've resorted to burying bodies without caskets since all the carpenters are sick and the warehouses have run out. The big cities are holding mass funerals in order to bury the corpses before they begin to putrefy. The courts are already swamped due to the lack of death certificates, causing problems for the surviving families. Boy howdy, what a god damn mess. I hope to hell the flu doesn't make it out to us here on the frontier."

Connal Lee clucked his tongue. "I hope not, too. I've had the flu before when I was a little kid. It's plumb miserable."

White Wolf looked Connal Lee in the eye. "I told you. Winter now time of sickness since the white man start travel through our hunting grounds. We lose people every winter to influenza. Some year more. Some year less. Awful way to die. No able breathe. Choke to death. We medicine men know no treatment. No herbs. No rituals. We feel helpless. We hate white man disease."

They all three shook their heads in dismay, then turned their attention to trading.

The last wagon train from St. Louis carrying trade goods had brought a lot of foods preserved in tin cans. Connal Lee bought canned ground coffee, canned tomatoes, and portable soups to augment their food supply. On an impulse, he purchased half a dozen cans of peaches to take back to the winter camp as a special treat for his family.

Shortly after six that evening, the three happy families arrived at the classroom door carrying dishes of food. Gilbert brought a large, hot apple pie in his gloved hands and placed it on the potbelly stove to stay hot until dessert. They shed their overcoats in the warmth from the heat stove and sat down to a feast.

Everyone admired the new dinner plates. Lorna heaped her praises and thanks on Zeff and Sister Woman for making them for her. Sister Woman helped Lorna dish up and serve soup in her new matching bowls. They chatted happily while they ate.

Zeff recounted his run-in with a giant black bear when going to the toilet by the river. They all laughed, imagining him running full out in a panic to retrieve his shotgun, holding his pants up as he ran. When he finished his tale, White Wolf glanced back and forth between Zeff and Connal Lee. "Both brother fight kill black bear. Brave family. Lucky family, too."

Of course, this meant Connal Lee had to tell the story once again of the Crow arrow in his leg and when he killed the yearling black bear cub attracted by the blood. He enjoyed lavishing his praise and thanks, once again, on White Wolf and Short Rainbow for caring for him and healing him.

They had nearly finished eating when they heard a brisk knock on the simple wood plank door. Lorna opened it. "Why, Mister Mackey, how nice of you to come calling. Won't you please come in and join us. I was just about to serve warm apple pie and coffee for dessert."

"Why, thank you. That's mighty nice of you, Missus Baines. I haven't had me any apple pie for ages."

They made room for Mr. Mackey to sit at the table. Lorna cut and served the pie. Sister Woman poured coffee and then set the coffee pot on the table. They all settled down and began eating dessert. Mr. Mackey smiled around at the table. "Thank you, everyone. This is certainly a nice family gathering, isn't it? Well, listen, we just received word a little while ago. The army convoy is due in around noon tomorrow. Captain Reed sent the fort another advance messenger. I thought you would like to know."

Connal Lee looked up with a happy grin. "Thanks, Mister Mackey. Ah was wondering when they would arrive. Now Ah can go out and greet them."

"The messenger happened to mention the convoy is carrying a small selection of school books and some novels to start a little lending library here at the trading post."

Lorna and Connal Lee looked at each other in delight. "That's great! Some new books to read. Ah can't wait!"

The next day, Connal Lee bundled up against the cold. He saddled his pretty mare and rode out to meet the convoy. The area hadn't received any more snow after the first two-foot snowfall. Since the temperature remained below freezing day and night, snow still covered the land. Breezes had created small undulating snowbanks like windblown desert sand. The powdery snow created no obstacle for livestock and wagons to travel through, but it made it difficult for the animals to find fodder.

Connal Lee spotted the army convoy ahead of him. The rising sun cast shadows in front of the riders and wagons. Connal Lee spurred his lovely brown filly to gallop towards them. Even from a distance, he recognized Captain Reed riding his magnificent stallion, Paragon. The Captain rode proudly at the head of the regiment guarding the lumbering wagon train, each heavily laden wagon pulled by a team of four great oxen. Connal Lee took off his muskrat fur hat and waved it in the air. Connal Lee watched Paragon jump into action and race towards him while the Captain waved his hat overhead.

They met on the trail, reined in their mounts, removed their fur-lined riding gauntlets, and vigorously shook hands. Big smiles on their faces showed their teeth. "Connal Lee! I was hoping you would turn up after I left. What happened to you after the Crow war party, anyway?"

"How have y'all been, Captain Reed, suh? It's so great to see y'all again. Ah was so happy to hear y'all were making another visit. How long are y'all staying this time? How has Paragon been on the long journey? Boy, that's sure a huge wagon train, isn't it, Captain?"

The captain chuckled as he waited for Connal Lee's questions to taper off so he could respond. "Well, Little Brother, I've been given command of the Fort. So, it appears I'll be here for a while. Come, ride beside me, and I'll tell you all about the transfer."

"What? Y'all are going to be living here a while? That's great! Yahoo!"

They rode at the head of the convoy. A few minutes later, Lieutenant Anderson galloped forward and joined them. "Connal Lee! You are safe after all. So nice to see you alive and kicking."

The three young men pulled over to the side of the trail and stopped their horses long enough for Connal Lee and the Lieutenant to shake hands. The wagon train lumbered noisily past them without pause. "Nice to see y'all, too, Lieutenant. Listen, my friends, to celebrate y'all arriving at the fort today, would y'all please join us for supper this evening? We have so much to talk about. We'll be eating in a tipi on the west side of the fort. It's the only tipi around, so y'all won't have any trouble finding it."

"What time will supper be served, Little Brother?"

"Please drop by around dusk."

131

They both accepted Connal Lee's invitation. Lieutenant Anderson turned his horse around. "Well, excuse me. I'll go back to my platoon. See you this evening, Connal Lee, Captain Reed, sir."

As they drew near the large wooden doors in the fort's tall adobe wall, Connal Lee followed the captain into the courtyard. Small log cabin buildings lined most of the defensive walls. Connal Lee saw a lieutenant walk out of the smaller two-story log cabins. Connal Lee and the captain dismounted and led their horses over to the hitching posts. The captain and lieutenant knew each other from serving together before. The lieutenant saluted Captain Reed and then shook his hand. "Welcome to Fort Hall, Captain Reed, sir. Come on in. Let me show you your new quarters, sir." The Lieutenant waved his arm towards the log cabin on the left. "Your office is on the ground floor, and your sleeping quarters are on the second floor. Let me show you, sir."

"Thank you. Lead on, Lieutenant Cooper."

Connal Lee decided he should leave the captain to settle into his new command. He pointed at the top of the tall tipi, showing above the fort's walls. "Well, Ah'll be off now, Captain. See y'all at supper in that tipi over there."

"I'll be there, Connal Lee. So long for now."

As Connal Lee rode out the gate, he nearly bumped into the captain's teenage slave boy, Ned, riding a spirited mare alongside a big Conestoga wagon. The teamster turned the plodding oxen to go through the gate. Ned stopped his mare and pushed his big felt hat up off his forehead. Connal Lee waved. "Ah sure am surprised to see y'all here, Ned. The captain brought y'all along with him, then?"

Ned grinned and shouted to be heard over the rumble of the wagon and the plodding oxen. "Yessuh. He needs lots of attention, our good Captain does. So does Paragon. Where did they go, suh, does y'all know?"

"Right through the gates. He's in the small two-story log cabin."

"Great. Thanks, suh. We done brought all 'is furniture with 'im. It's in that there big wagon. Ah've gotta get busy now an' get 'im unpacked. Why we even has us a potbelly stove fer 'is bedroom."

Ned turned and led his mare through the gates, still grinning.

"Wow. The Captain sure does live fancy, doesn't he? Well. Good luck, Ned. See y'all around, then."

"Yessuh."

That evening, as darkness settled over the Fort, the captain and lieutenant walked to the tipi together. They saw a wisp of smoke drifting out of the smoke hole at the top and heard voices inside. Not knowing the polite way to announce their arrival since the tipi didn't have a door upon which to knock, Captain Reed called out, "Ahoy the tipi. Connal Lee, are you in there?"

Connal Lee pushed aside the doeskin door and waved from where he stood inside the egg-shaped opening. "Captain. Lieutenant. Come on in. Glad y'all could make it. Please come in out of the cold. Welcome. Welcome."

The tall men ducked down and entered the tipi. Connal Lee pulled the door back over the hole and tied it with a small braid of rawhide. Then he lowered the leather inner lining that helped insulate the interior from the stark winter cold. "Here, let me take your coats and hats, gentlemen. Y'all won't need them in here."

Connal Lee placed them behind the inner leather tent lining beside the doorway. Captain Reed saw how Connal Lee's family stored all their everyday items neatly tucked out of the way. He found it a clever way to keep the mess out of sight while efficiently using space too low to stand under. "Why, thank you, Connal Lee."

Everyone stood up to greet the new arrivals. The captain and lieutenant walked over and began shaking hands. "Mister and Missus Swinton, it's so good to see you again."

"Y'all, too, Captain, Lieutenant. Welcome tuh Fort Hall."

"Mister and Missus Baines. A pleasure to see you again as well. You were such a help with our wounded on the Trail that we think of you as friends."

"We were thrilled to hear the two of you would be visiting the fort. We are delighted to see you, both."

Connal Lee walked over and put his arm around Short Rainbow's shoulders. "Gentlemen, may Ah present my wife, Short Rainbow, a niece of Chief Arimo. She is studying to become a healer in the shaman tradition. Short Rainbow, this is my best friend and oldest foster brother, Captain John Reed from Boston, and my other good friend, Lieutenant Lucas Anderson."

Neither man could hide his astonishment.

Connal Lee stepped over and rested his hand affectionately on Screaming Eagle's muscled shoulder. "And this is my brother husband Screaming Eagle, Chief Arimo's nephew and apprentice War Chief." He placed his other hand on White Wolf's shoulder and drew him closer. "And this is my other brother husband, White Wolf, another of Chief Arimo's nephews. He is becoming a medicine man. He saved my life after Ah was wounded by a Crow war arrow and later wounded by a black bear drawn to the smell of my blood as Ah lay wounded on the ground."

Connal Lee let go of his spouses' shoulders and pointed at Bright Star. "Gentlemen, this is Bright Star, Short Rainbow's youngest sister, who is traveling with us this trip." She bounced over and stood on her toes as she solemnly shook their hands. "How do you do? How do you do?"

Her cheerfulness charmed both men. Captain Reed shook her hand with a big smile. "I am doing well. It's a pleasure to meet you, my dear."

Connal Lee used both hands to gesture at two seats made of neatly folded buffalo hides. "We made these fur sleeping blankets to welcome y'all to our home and to the frontier. They are from my family and me. If ya sleep on top of one blanket and under the second, y'all will be warm no matter if it's in a bed or out on the open ground."

Connal Lee crossed his ankles and gracefully sank down between the captain and the lieutenant's fur cushion seats. Everyone sat down Indian-style on the floor covered with pelts. Lorna Baines chuckled with her hand politely covering her mouth. "You should have seen your faces when Connal Lee introduced his wife and husbands. I swear both your jaws hit the floor at the same time."

Everyone joined her, laughing and pointing. The Captain took the ribbing all in good nature. He smiled and nodded his head towards her. "Well, Missus Baines, it is a lot to take in, isn't it?" He then glanced over at Connal Lee. "Well, Little Brother, you have really grown up on the trail since we met months ago back in Fort Laramie, haven't you? Taller. More mature. More muscular. Neatly dressed.

Clean. Your hair cut and combed. Speaking proper English. Very impressive, young man. And married, too! My lord, I certainly never expected that."

Connal Lee blushed. "Ah didn't either, Captain Reed. But after they saved my life, we all became good friends. Then we all just sort of fell in love with each other. It's the best thing that ever happened to me in my whole life. Now we all fit together like we were always meant to be. Destiny, Ah believe they call it. And fate, too."

Lorna winked at Connal Lee, smiling approvingly at his proper use of new vocabulary. Lieutenant Anderson gazed around at the spacious interior of the tipi. Short Rainbow had lit the tipi with four tallow candles hung high overhead in addition to the small fire burning for warmth. "This is much bigger on the inside than it looks, isn't it? Short Rainbow, your tipi makes a lovely home. Thank you for letting us visit it."

Captain Reed agreed. "I've seen plenty of tipis on the frontier, but this is the first time I've been invited to enter one. I'm surprised it is so spacious, so clean, and so comfortable. Now, Little Brother, I'm dying of curiosity to hear what happened to you after you became separated from the handcart company this side of the divide. Everyone was worried to death about you."

Connal Lee leaned over and rested his elbows on his knees. "Well, suh. A lot happened."

While Connal Lee told of his adventures and how his Shoshone family saved his life, the ladies took that as their opportunity to serve supper. They raised the inner tent lining, lifted out plates, and placed one in front of each person without saying a word. Between them, they barely had enough forks for everyone. Then they pulled out platters of venison steaks, fried grouse, fresh bread, and bowls of mashed potatoes, pemmican, and stewed fruits. The wives passed the food around and served everyone. They enjoyed a convivial and lively conversation with lots of exclamations.

"You don't say!"

"Really? Amazing."

"Good lord, Connal Lee!"

Connal Lee enjoyed watching their faces as he told about meeting Brigham Young, the head of the Mormon Church and Governor of the

Territory of Utah. He related how he had to travel back to Fort Hall to find Zeff and Sister Woman, homesteading a clay claim a few miles north of the Fort.

As everyone finished eating, Short Rainbow gracefully whisked away their plates and forks, cleaning up the floor of her home. Lorna brought out a tin pie pan of rich chocolate brownies and served everyone a piece to hold in their hands. "Mm. Mother Baines, this is the best yet. Captain Reed, Mother Baines now has a cookstove with an oven in her cabin in the school building. She's the fort's unofficial baker. The men garrisoned here treasure her already. Plus, she's the new teacher here at the Fort. Isn't she incredible?"

After they enjoyed the brownies, Short Rainbow passed around a moist piece of soft chamois cloth to clean their fingers. Connal Lee licked his fingers clean before the washcloth reached him.

Everyone shared their stories about building a home in the side of a cliff and building a brick kiln, about living a short while in Fort Bountiful, of surviving measles in Chief Arimo's winter camp down on the Portneuf River, of being adopted by Chief Arimo, of learning to sew on a treadle sewing machine. The hour grew late. The captain covered a yawn and shook his head. "Amazing. So much has happened in your lives. Such progress. Adventures, even. I'm happy for all of you. My life has just been the daily routines of training new recruits, drilling my troops, riding patrol, and guarding the Overland Trail. But all of you have had exciting experiences.

"Connal Lee, I'm pleased to see you growing up so nicely. Well, everyone. This has been a most pleasant evening. Thank you so much for inviting us. It was very nice seeing and meeting everyone. Well, it's been a long day on horseback. I'm ready to head back to my quarters and get some rest. Zeff, please come see me tomorrow about a brick foundation for a new watermill. Good night, everyone."

When the Captain stood up, everyone else did, too. Connal Lee helped the Captain into his overcoat. When he handed the Captain his hat, Connal Lee leaned in and gave him a hug. "Thanks for the gift of The Three Musketeers. It's a wonderful book. Thanks for thinking of me."

Short Rainbow bounced over and handed the Captain his two heavy buffalo blankets.

Connal Lee also hugged the Lieutenant after he helped him into his long wool coat. "Thanks, Lieutenant, for Nicholas Nickleby. What a great book. Thanks very much."

"You are entirely welcome, Connal Lee. So nice to see you again. Good night."

White Wolf handed the Lieutenant his sleeping furs. They both nodded and smiled at each other. Connal Lee lifted up the tent lining and pushed open the doeskin door so his guests could leave. Before he could shut the door, Lorna and Gilbert had pulled on their coats and said their goodbyes, followed quickly by Zeff and Sister Woman carrying a sleeping Chester Ray in her arms. Everyone shared hugs and kisses all around. Finally, peace and quiet descended around Connal Lee's loving family.

After breakfast the following day, Connal Lee and White Wolf helped Zeff and Sister Woman take down the new tent and pack it up neatly for transportation. Connal Lee recommended that Zeff and Sister Woman take the tent and store it at their little home. "We usually spend the night with y'all when we are up to the Fort, so the tent might as well be stored with y'all for convenience."

They lifted the heavy bundle of the tent onto the back of Zeff's mule-drawn handcart. "We'll be glad tuh store the tent, Little Brover. Come see us soon. Bye fer now!"

"Happy trails, Big Brover."

Following is a preview of the continuation
of Connal Lee's adventures in

PIONEER SPIRIT
Book Three: Wars and Rumors

Available now in paperback and on Kindle

Chapter 1: Christmas

After hosting Connal Lee's family reunion to celebrate the arrival of Captain Reed and Lieutenant Anderson at Fort Hall, Connal Lee and his spouses packed up Short Rainbow's tipi. They rode south to Chief SoYo'Cant's winter camp, where they settled in for the duration of the winter.

After supper that evening, White Wolf pulled Bright Star in to sit beside him with his arm around her shoulder. She blushed a little but snuggled up to his side. Connal Lee let his instincts guide him. He crawled over on hands and knees and laid down beside Short Rainbow. He reached out and began caressing her pert breasts before leaning over and giving her a lingering kiss. Screaming Eagle quickly joined in. He reached over and pulled Connal Lee's doeskin shirt up and off his arms. Then he began undressing Short Rainbow while Connal Lee untied his leggings and removed his loincloth. Soon, clothes flew everywhere as they rushed to get naked, laughing at their enthusiasm and impatience.

No one had played with Bright Star during their short journey to Fort Hall and back. Gently, White Wolf helped her remove her leggings and beaded smock. He quickly slipped off his clothes and then sat against one of the beaded sling chair backs suspended from a tent pole. He reached out and pulled Bright Star to rest against him, snuggling her bare back against his naked torso. Her head fell back to rest on his shoulder. White Wolf wrapped his arms around her just below her tiny breasts, humming his pleasure and contentment to finally feel her smooth, lithe body in his arms. He leaned down and kissed her cheek, then her lips. Bright Star wrapped her arms over White Wolf's and snuggled back.

On the other side of the tipi, Connal Lee entered Short Rainbow. They began actively thrusting and withdrawing, sharing their bodies and joy with each other. Screaming Eagle scrounged around under the inner tipi lining until he found the small clay jar White Wolf had filled with a slick ointment. They used it when Screaming Eagle wanted to make love to White Wolf more intimately. With his left hand, he anointed his straining erection until slippery. With his right hand, he caressed and smoothed the oily mixture over and into Connal Lee's exposed rear end. With a fierce look of total concentration, Screaming Eagle positioned his hard cock. He timed it carefully until Connal Lee began withdrawing, then slowly shoved in. He heard Connal Lee moan loudly. Whenever Connal Lee pushed into Short Rainbow, he pulled away from his husband's swollen member, joyfully milking it. When he pulled out of Short Rainbow, he thrust himself back on Screaming Eagle's strong masculinity. Soon all three moaned in pleasure.

Bright Star had watched couples copulating before, but this felt different, much more intimate and arousing. Her eyes grew wider as she watched, wondering when she would finally experience lovemaking as a grown woman. She felt White Wolf's penis grow erect behind her back. She snuggled in closer with a little wriggle, increasing their contact. White Wolf didn't want to rush her or push her into anything she didn't find pleasurable, but he found it harder and harder not to be a more active participant. They avidly enjoyed the erotic show before them. Connal Lee began sweating from his athletic exertions. Short Rainbow smiled enchantingly. She reached up and grabbed Screaming Eagle's long braids, then pulled his face down beside Connal Lee's so she could take turns kissing her beloved husbands while they rutted over her.

Slowly, lightly, White Wolf allowed his right hand to drift down Bright Star's slender stomach until his fingers reached between her legs. He began softly tickling and teasing her, seeking out that special sensitive nub all women enjoyed. His left hand began stroking her nipples, massaging her breasts until she writhed in his arms from the loving attack on two fronts. Before she expected it, Bright Star shuddered through her first orgasm at a man's hands, moaning, "Oh, White Wolf. What you do to me! It makes me melt in happiness."

Connal Lee and his partners heard her. They glanced over, delighted at the blissful look on her face. They watched while White Wolf thrust his erection against Bright Star's lean back as he hugged her closer, tighter, and more sensuously. Finally, he reached his ecstatic conclusion. As he relaxed, he pulled Bright Star down to cuddle beside him on their sleeping furs. He spent several minutes kissing

Bright Star's face, neck, eyes, and lips as they came down from their erotic highs.

The lusty trio pressed on to their athletic conclusions without an audience. The men collapsed over Short Rainbow until she gave them a hard shove. "I can't breathe, you great heavy beasts. Roll over!"

Screaming Eagle reluctantly withdrew from Connal Lee's slick warmth. He collapsed on his left side and stretched out beside Short Rainbow. Connal Lee had already gone soft, so he just rolled over to her right side. He leaned on his elbow so he could kiss Short Rainbow. His hand reached out and grabbed Screaming Eagle's bulging bicep and gave it a squeeze. "I love y'all, Short Rainbow. I love y'all Screaming Eagle."

They all cuddled up in a pile to sleep.

A week later, Connal Lee visited the fort leading two pack horses loaded with trading furs. Even though below freezing, he found it a beautiful day for riding. The briskness made him feel vital and strong, breathing the crisp, clean air and soaking up the mild radiant heat from the sun rising on his right. Connal Lee invited Captain Reed to return with him to his adopted father's winter quarters. "I think it's time for you to meet the great Chief Arimo, John. You can stay with us in our family's snug tipi."

After Connal Lee introduced the captain to Chief SoYo'Cant that evening, they accepted the Chief's invitation to stay for supper in his tipi. Later that night, they returned to Short Rainbow's tipi. The captain spread his buffalo skin blankets alongside Connal Lee's distinctive red fox fur blanket. They all sat around the small hardwood fire that warmed the big tent, making small talk and enjoying the captain's company.

Later that night, Connal Lee pulled the captain into his happy family as they all made love together.

While they ate breakfast, Lieutenant Cooper approached the camp from the north, riding his stallion hard. Shoshone Warriors became alarmed and intercepted him before he reached their encampment. The Lieutenant reined in his steaming horse and raised his arm in the sign of peace and friend. "Peace."

The warriors returned the sign and greeted him, "Peace."

Thinking he now had permission to enter the encampment and impatient to deliver his report to Captain Reed, he kicked his stallion and started to ride around the guards. They stopped him, again, with raised hands. "No! Stop!"

The excited Lieutenant called out in a loud voice, thinking if he spoke loudly enough, it would force the men blocking his way to understand him. "I need to report to Captain Reed right away. Let me by. Where is Captain Reed?"

One of the warriors spoke enough English to catch his drift. He pointed his finger to the center of the camp. "Go Chief SoYo'Cant. Now. Go!"

The Lieutenant saw he would need permission from Chief Arimo before he could deliver his message, so he agreed. "Please lead the way. I go to Chief Arimo, now."

The English-speaking warrior turned his big palomino stallion around and trotted back to the large encampment. A few minutes later, they approached the chief's outdoor council chamber. The lieutenant leapt off his horse, faced the Chief, and gave him a crisp military salute. The chief rose to his feet and made the sign of peace. Lieutenant Cooper returned the peace sign. Chief SoYo'Cant pointed at him. "Who you?"

"I am First Lieutenant Brandon Cooper of the First Contingent of Mounted Riflemen, Company G, Sixth Infantry, presently stationed in Fort Hall under the orders of Captain Reed, sir."

He pulled a thin leather satchel off a long leather strap over his shoulder and held it towards the chief. "I come bearing emergency communiques from Major Sanderson, commander of Fort Laramie and of all the Overland Trail. May I please have your permission to deliver my messages, sir?"

"Welcome. I Chief Arimo. Go. Warrior Yo-ko-ap lead way." The chief pointed at the warrior who had led the Lieutenant into the camp. "Lead this young cavalry officer to Short Rainbow's tipi, Yo-ko-ap, right away. He has important business with Captain Reed."

The imperious warrior leapt onto his horse's back, then turned and beckoned to Lieutenant Cooper. "Come."

The Lieutenant nodded his thanks to the chief and rushed over to mount up and follow. Within moments they arrived at Short Rainbow's tipi, where they found everyone sitting around the cookfire finishing their breakfast. When the captain spotted his first lieutenant riding quickly towards them, he stood up in alarm. Yo-ko-ap called ahead, "Screaming Eagle! Chief SoYo'Cant ordered me to deliver this pale face to your friend Chief Fort Hall."

Screaming Eagle stood up as they approached the campfire. "Thank you, Yo-ko-ap."

Connal Lee stood up next to the captain and translated. The captain made the sign of peace to Yo-ko-ap with a polite nod. "Thank you."

Captain Reed watched his lieutenant dismount. White Wolf strode over to Lieutenant Cooper. "Here. I take horse."

The lieutenant nodded. "Thank you." Turning, he stood at attention before Captain Reed and saluted. He then jerked the leather satchel off his shoulder and held it out to the captain. "Captain Reed, sir. Late last night, a rush courier arrived from Fort Laramie. He handed me this dispatch containing a copy of an army intelligence report forwarded with orders from Major Sanderson."

"Thank you, Lieutenant. At ease. Please have some coffee while I read the dispatches."

The captain resumed his seat beside the fireplace. He unfastened the leather belts securing the thin message bag, and removed several folded pieces of paper. He shook them out and began reading. It took him twenty minutes to study the long intelligence report and read the major's orders.

When he set the papers down on the satchel, Connal Lee leaned forward and stared at the captain, anxious to hear the news. The captain sat silently for several minutes, digesting everything he had read. Then he glanced around at Connal Lee and his family. "Would you please accompany me to visit Chief Arimo? I believe he should know about the events described in this report I just received from the Military Intelligence Division of Army Headquarters back in West Point."

Everyone stood up. Screaming Eagle led them directly to the Chief's outdoor council chamber. After they exchanged warm greetings, Connal Lee took charge. "Father SoYo'Cant, Captain Reed receive important message from United States of America government. He want you know what happen."

"Thank you, son. Please, everyone, take a seat while I send for Teniwaaten to translate for me."

Connal Lee waved his family to sit around the blazing fire. The captain understood and joined them. When Teniwaaten arrived, the Chief introduced him to Captain Reed. The captain stood up to shake hands. "Can you translate my message for Chief Arimo, please?"

"It's nice to make your acquaintance, Captain Reed. It would be my pleasure, sir."

"Would it be easier for me to read it out loud, and then you translate, or would it be easier for you to read and translate it directly for yourself?"

"If the hand of the writer of the message is clear to my eyes, it will be faster if I read and translate. Please sit next to me so you can clarify it for me if I can't make out a word."

"Very well. Here is the report. Please let me know when I can be of help."

Teniwaaten sat down beside his chief and patted the ground on his other side. The captain sat down with his legs crossed, Indian style. "Teniwaaten, before you start, please let the Chief know that this is a report of the political situation back in the Federal Capital. It also contains a copy of the orders sent to Colonel Johnston's army. All the information refers to the Utah problem and how the president and congress are handling the crisis."

Teniwaaten began translating. An hour later, he finished the intelligence report. Everyone around the council fire waited respectfully for their revered chieftain to respond. The chief thought about what he had learned and finally turned to Teniwaaten. "Please ask Captain Reed for his evaluation of these developments. What does he think it means for us and our Mormon allies?"

Since the conversation began in Shoshone, Captain Reed had been thinking of nothing else. He looked Chief SoYo'Cant in the eye. "Well, sir. Most of the news is favorable, although it still leaves Salt Lake Valley highly vulnerable to invasion. I didn't like hearing about orders to bring the invading army back north along the Oregon Trail and then south through our lands here rather than going directly southwest on the Mormon Trail, which was their original path. Of course, it will delay them as they will have to travel north to the trail, then west, then back south, again, from Fort Hall. However, the approaching winter season might help us. It's so late in the year, the mountain passages are bound to be unpassable due to snow and below-freezing temperatures."

The Chief nodded his agreement. "I liked hearing about the Mormon's allies in the senate and how unpopular this war has become with Congress. I am glad Congress keeps delaying funding the president's requests for more money to pursue this unpopular war. It is good that the newspapers report how badly things are going with this military mission. The one item of greatest concern to me is the report of sending reinforcements to Colonel Johnston that would bring his force up to five-thousand armed men."

After listening to the translation, Captain Reed nodded his agreement. "Yes, sir. That would place Johnston in command of one-third of the entire armed forces of the United States, five full battalions. It will take some time for the men to meet up with Colonel Johnston, especially this time of year. Perhaps of more immediate concern was Johnston's promotion to Brevet Brigadier General. That will give him a lot of influence at central command and make him one of America's most powerful field officers. Only a handful of Major Generals now outrank him."

The chief scowled. "Yes. Very bad news about five battalions of men directed towards the Mormons and the rest of us who also live in these territories. Do you know this Albert Sidney Johnston, Captain Reed?"

"No, sir. I have never met him. However, I know him by reputation. I understand he is from Kentucky. He is a graduate of West Point. He owns an enormous plantation on the southeast coast of Texas, south of Houston. He has so many slaves he runs a school for their children on his plantation. He's a very progressive thinker and strategist. He has fought Cherokees and Mexicans in the Texian Army. After he helped liberate Texas from Mexico, he served as Secretary of War for the Republic of Texas for several years. Then he fought in the Mexican-American war. He is very experienced in leading men and very aggressive in pursuing his military objectives. He's strictly a by-the-book man in following his orders."

Teniwaaten hesitated, then glanced over at the captain. "Captain Reed, what does 'by-the-book' mean?"

"Oh. It means adhering strictly to the exact wording of an order no matter what extenuating circumstances might arise."

"Ah, yes. I understand."

After Teniwaaten translated, the Chief looked Captain Reed in the eye. "I think Chief Brigham Young should know of these political maneuverings in the Federal Capital and of the planned increase in troops heading our way. What do you think, captain?"

"I concur, sir. I was thinking much the same thing. I can dispatch riders to deliver the intelligence to Governor Young immediately."

The chief shook his head no. "Federal soldiers riding to Great Salt Lake City are bound to be delayed if not stopped outright. What if we send Screaming Eagle's family with Connal Lee to translate. The Mormons still allow us, their allies, into their forts."

Captain Reed thought about it, then nodded his agreement. "That might be for the best. If they each took three horses so they could change mounts as needed, they could cover a lot of ground in a hurry. They wouldn't need to take much in the way of provisions. If they are willing to accept this mission, I believe it would be the best course of action."

The suggestion excited Connal Lee. His family listened most attentively as Teniwaaten translated for their chief. Chief SoYo'Cant leaned forward and peered into the faces of his nieces and nephews. "Will you accept my orders to ride south at all possible speed to deliver this information to Chief Brigham Young?"

They all nodded their heads eagerly. "Yes, Chief SoYo'Cant."

Connal Lee leapt to his feet. "Yes, Father SoYo'Cant. If White Wolf and I rode out immediately, we could return by nightfall with our family's army surplus tent for shelter during the night. Screaming Eagle, Short Rainbow, and Bright Star could organize the horses and supplies while we fetched the tent. We could leave at first light tomorrow morning."

The chief looked back at Captain Reed. They both nodded their heads, approving Connal Lee's plan. The captain stood up. "I will ride back to Fort Hall with you, Connal Lee. While you ride on to Zeff's homestead to pick up your tent, I will copy the report for my records so I can study it further. You can pick up the original on your way back here and take it along to Governor Young."

Everyone stood up. The Chief shook hands with Captain Reed. "Good. Thank you."

The captain pointed to Connal Lee and White Wolf. "Let's mount up and be on our way."

Everyone scattered to their duties. As the captain walked beside Connal Lee, he asked if he could borrow another horse so he could change horses midway. Connal Lee helped him cut out one of his large Crow victory horses, about the same size as Paragon, from the clan's general herd. As they saddled up, the captain recommended they ride at a trot the entire way.

Connal Lee and his family arose before dawn. They ate a hot breakfast, saddled their horses, and loaded their provisions. At six-thirty, they took off riding south, alternating every half hour between a trot and a cantor. They stopped for a short rest every four hours and ate a cold meal standing up. The temperatures never rose above fifty degrees but fortunately stayed above freezing that night. They moved their saddles and supplies to fresh horses and rode for another four hours. The horses made too much noise for conversation. By the end of the third four-hour segment of their journey, the horses and humans began lagging. They slept like logs after eating a satisfying supper of stew made from dried meats, vegetables, and herbs.

On Friday morning, the twenty-fifth of December, Short Rainbow and Bright Star prepared a hearty, hot breakfast before sunrise. The men saddled the horses and loaded up the tent and travel provisions. By dawn, they continued their exhausting, mile-eating pace. They rode up to the west gate of Great Salt Lake City around nine-thirty that morning. A small group of volunteer civilian guards challenged them. Connal Lee pulled ahead to greet them. "Peace. I am Connal Lee Swinton, the adopted son of Chief Arimo. Chief Arimo and Captain Reed, the commander of Fort Hall, ordered us to deliver important military intelligence to Governor Young at the best possible speed. Please let us through to the Beehive House."

The guards recognized the Shoshone family as allies and waved them through with calls of merry Christmas. Connal Lee and his family followed Screaming Eagle with all their horses directly to Beehive House. After they tied up their fifteen saddle horses and six pack-horses, Connal Lee took charge. He marched up and knocked briskly on the door in the massive wall, decorated with a four-foot-wide pine wreath. An oversized bow of cotton cloth dyed bright red tied the branches into a circle. The same middle-aged women who had greeted them on their last visit recognized them. Clutching a heavy shawl around her shoulders, she pushed open the heavy gate. "Good morning, and Merry Christmas to you all. Please come in where it's warm." She led the way up the porch. "By the way, we didn't introduce ourselves when you were here last month. I'm Mary Ann Angell Young, Brigham's wife. I'm called either Mother Young or Sister Young. And you are?"

After they walked through the mansion's front door, Connal Lee introduced everyone, ending with himself. "We are a delegation sent by Captain Reed of Fort Hall and Chief Arimo of the Shoshone Nation with important intelligence for Governor Young."

"Please wait here a moment while I inform him of your arrival. He returned a few minutes ago from his church office next door and immediately sat down to consult with officers of the Nauvoo Legion." She pointed to a large oak hall tree with a narrow mirror in its middle panel. "You may leave your coats, capes, and weapons here in the entrance, then wait in the parlor, please. I will be right back."

"Thanks, Sister Young."

Connal Lee gazed around at the Christmas decorations with garlands of pine branches over the doors and windows, even over the hall tree. A fragrant pine tree stood in front of the parlor's window overlooking the street, decorated with chains of popped corn and dried red and purple berries. Garlands of dried flowers added a touch of color. Each window held a candle sitting on the sill in a simple brass candlestick.

Within minutes, Connal Lee watched a parade of six uniformed officers march out of Brigham Young's office. Mrs. Young ushered in the Shoshone delegation. They shook hands with Governor Young, introduced Bright Star, and exchanged Christmas wishes. Brigham Young invited them to take the recently vacated chairs already placed in a half-circle before his desk. "Now, what's this about bringing me important military intelligence?"

Connal Lee leaned forward and recapped the events of the past two and a half days, then stood up. He lifted the army dispatch bag off his shoulder and placed it on the desk. They watched as the Governor opened it and withdrew the packet of papers. He looked up at Connal Lee and then gazed around at his Shoshone family. "Thank you for bringing this to me so swiftly. Is there anything I can get you to eat or drink? This will take me a few minutes to read."

"No thanks, Governor. We ate breakfast this morning. We are here to await y'all's orders, suh."

Brigham Young nodded, put on his reading glasses, and focused on the report. When he finished, the Governor leaned back in his big leather desk chair. "I want to share this information with some of my key officers, Master Connal Lee." He looked at the small wall clock opposite his desk, amazed it wasn't even ten o'clock. "Please let me invite you and your delegation to return in two hours to join me for a Christmas luncheon at midday. We can discuss our plans, and I will prepare missives for you to return to our good ally, Chief Arimo, and to Captain Reed. If you will excuse me, I have a lot to do."

Connal Lee led his family out to the street. They decided to take advantage of the time to erect their tent. They set up camp beside the Jordan River, where the Chief had made camp on their last visit. They expected to at least be there overnight.

After a delicious meal of roasted goose served with roasted vegetables, the portly governor sat back in his chair at the head of the table. "Please give me a half-hour or so. I would like to write letters to Chief Arimo and Captain Reed for you to take back with you. You may rest here or walk outside as you please."

When Brigham Young stood up, they all did. Connal Lee looked at his family. White Wolf indicated for them to remain in the warm dining room. Connal Lee shook hands with the Governor. "We can be found here whenever y'all are ready for us, suh. Thanks very much for the kind hospitality and the delicious meal, Your Honor. Merry Christmas, suh."

The Governor nodded his agreement, then strode briskly out the door. After Connal Lee and his family resumed their chairs, two of Brigham Young's daughters brought them plates of gingerbread and sugar cookies with red and green icing. A young servant girl from the kitchen carried in a fresh pot of hot chocolate and a bowl of peppermint candies. They all adored the sweets. Brigham Young returned at two-thirty and handed Connal Lee the messenger packet. "Thank you for your services to my people. Please extend our thanks to the chief and the captain for keeping us abreast of important developments. I already expressed my gratitude in the letters in this pouch, but please reinforce our appreciation for their thoughtfulness and your kind services. Goodbye for now. Safe trails and a very merry Christmas to you all."

They shook hands and departed for their camp. An hour later, they had packed up and took off, heading north. They rode at a steady trot covering around eight miles an hour all the way back, changing horses when they sensed them tiring. They arrived at Short Rainbow's tipi late the afternoon of their second day. White Wolf suggested Screaming Eagle find them some fresh meat for supper. Their marathon trip left them all tired and hungry for a hot meal. The young family tended their weary horses. As soon as they finished, White Wolf pointed to the center of the encampment. "I think Connal Lee and I should go deliver Governor Young's letter to Uncle SoYo'Cant right away. Tomorrow morning, Connal Lee and I will ride to Fort Hall and deliver the governor's letter to Captain Reed."

That evening, Chief SoYo'Cant expressed his thanks for a speedy and successful mission.

Connal Lee and White Wolf joined Captain Reed for his midday meal at Fort Hall the following day. The captain also thanked them, congratulating them on the successful conclusion of their first diplomatic mission. "Well done, gentlemen. Well done, indeed."

Made in the USA
Monee, IL
06 September 2023

42229490R00090